And Then There's Carrie

And Then There's Carrie

Phyllis Levine

Loconeal Select

Amherst, Ohio

And Then There's Carrie

Published by Loconeal Select. Loconeal Select books can be ordered through booksellers, Ingram, or by contacting: sales@loconeal.com * www.loconeal.com * 216-772-8380

ISBN: Softcover   978-1-940466-25-5   November 2014

This book was printed in the United States of America.

Other books by Phyllis Levine

The Alphabet Beach Song
Small Pleasures (Poetry)
Matilda
At the Skylight with Matilda
Matilda's Way
What's up Matilda?

Quote

"Patience and passage of time do more than strength and fury."
Jean de la Fontaine

For my family

Preface

Dear Readers,

Many of you have read my first book titled Matilda, and followed it with the series. A main character in the series is Carrie, Matilda's best friend. Carrie takes the lead in this book and is shocked to hear that Matilda has changed her lifestyle too fast, so now Carrie questions whether to continue to support Matilda. Carrie presents her views and opinions about her longtime friend Matilda. She has much to say about the culture and society. Carrie is tired of nasty looks because of the way she dresses, and ignores cutting remarks. After all she is her own person!

Meet many of the characters from the Matilda series. They have much to say. There's Anne Wiggins and Ron Rosen, along with some new ones who try to make good decisions. Will they work? As for Carrie, she has lots to think about and learn.

Sincerely,
Phyllis Levine

One

The News

Carrie Adler hit her mobile phone button to off. A puzzled expression swept over her face, and the lights in her eyes that were bright with anticipation a few moments ago transformed into a dazed gloom. The message she had heard concerned Matilda, her best friend, who was about to change her life. In hearing this announcement from Matilda's mother, the phone slid from Carrie's hand on to the kitchen floor. In her small London flat, Carrie gasped, retrieved her phone and screamed.

"Oh, no, it's broken," she wailed. Plugging the phone in an outlet above her kitchen counter, she pushed a button and an old message sprung forth. "Great, it works after all," sighed Carrie, making a mental image to remember where to locate her most important connection to the world.

In the past six months, Carrie had lost two mobile phones. One had fallen out of the back pocket of her shorts into the toilet bowl. Aghast, she had dragged it out, glared, pouted, and then dumped it. With the second phone, she thought she had accidently dropped it among the produce section of the grocery store while sorting out crisp red apples with no blemishes. She had been chatting with a friend about nothing much, so couldn't remember if she had tucked the phone in her handbag pocket after the conversation ended.

Having left a Barnett store, established throughout London, where one could buy groceries, fresh sandwiches, pastries, the finest chocolates, and smart clothes all at a decent price, she had stopped walking. For a moment, she stood there questioning herself. Had she put her phone back in her bag? Opening the top zipper, she emptied out her valuables and rapidly searched, but the phone was missing. Cringing, she had rushed back to the store. Reaching the produce section, she filtered through the apples, and asked a busy clerk unloading bananas from a cardboard box if he had spotted a mobile phone, but he shrugged his shoulders and said no. Carrie shuddered, for she knew she would need to dip into her savings and purchase another phone. She had owned the two just a few months. Relieved that her third phone sat on her kitchen counter in good order, a contented smile crept over her face. It was then she returned to her waiting Sunday chores.

Most times, Carrie's inquisitive personality suggested fun and adventure, and not much upset her. When the phone rang, she had been gathering up old jeans, shirts, tops, shoes, and magazines to recycle at the Salvation Army. Throughout the week she had ignored the piled up accumulation of clothing stacked in the corner in her living room, which she had meant to sort out and stuff in a large plastic bag and deliver on Saturday, but had not done so.

"Oh, there's so much to do over the weekend if only I could catch up," she whined. Lifting her laundry basket from the scratched Formica kitchen counter, she marched to her bedroom and dumped the basket on her bed. She stacked away lingerie and accessories in an old walnut chest, and on a chair by her bedside she placed clothes for her Monday morning rush to get ready for work.

She had tried to become more organized and to be on time for her job and appointments, but somehow got delayed by changing outfits, redoing her hair, or deciding to do something which could possibly wait, which resulted in damaged relationships. But with this new job she forced herself to stay on task. In doing so, she dragged herself out of bed when the alarm went off at six-thirty am, but not without moaning and pulling the blanket over her head for a few extra minutes of sleep.

Satisfied with the chore completed, she placed her hands on her waist. "This is too much. It can't be happening. Can it?" she yelled, waving her arms in the air like a policewoman directing traffic on a busy highway. "What's with Matilda now? I can't understand her."

Leaving her bedroom, Carrie opened her pet Budgie's bird cage that stood in the living room. "Come on, my love, it's time to get you some exercise," she announced in an upbeat voice.

Pete flew around the room, finally settling on Carrie's outstretched index finger. Kissing him on his head, she put him into his cage. "That does it for you little one. Are you hungry?" she asked, placing some fresh seed in Pete's dish. "Looks like you're fine," she said, watching him.

Rain pounded against the front window, leaving heavy drops smothering the view. An odor of dampness hung in the air of her tiny flat which Carrie had tried to conceal with a perfumed spray, which she used frequently. She wanted to paint the small rooms in a variety of colors, but hadn't found the spare time to work on the project. Her landlord had said he would provide the paint. Approaching the window, she stared at the darkened sky and dull gray brick buildings.

"Why does it have to rain on Sunday?" she moaned. Spotting a man wearing a yellow plastic raincoat hurrying by and holding an umbrella close to his head, she sighed. "Damn," she said, turning to face her tennis racket that lay on a chair. "It's so nasty. I won't be playing in this! All it does is rain, and August is almost over. Oh, how I wish I could travel back to Miami Beach and lie in the sun, swim in the ocean, gather sea shells, dance all night, and find romance with a stranger like those old romance films that my mother watches and talks about constantly. Oh, my God, Matilda will no longer have a rich husband or live by the ocean. She's gone and left Mark Rosen and is getting a divorce! She traveled to Ohio to attend that fancy nanny school to become a nanny, married a wealthy man, and has now left him. Is she mad? It's only been a year since she wed. Anne said she'll probably marry Richard Evergreen. It doesn't make sense. What lousy news for Anne to tell me this morning. What's going on with my best friend? Is she thinking straight?"

Standing in the middle of her tiny living room, a sharp pain gripped her stomach. Stumbling into the kitchen, she grabbed the back of a chair. Letting go, she crawled to the bathroom. Trembling, she pulled herself up and clung to the counter. Not sure what had happened, she opened the medicine cabinet, located a bottle of nonprescription medication for an upset stomach, filled a glass of cold water, and downed two pills. Pulling out her painted white antique iron chair designed for a porch or patio, she sat down.

On a sunny Saturday afternoon, she had wandered about a consignment shop, and saw a rusty chair. She fell in love with it and bought it, knowing she shouldn't have with only a few pounds left in her checking account. Painting the chair white, and finding a purple pillow to adorn it, she stuck it in her bathroom. It gave her bathroom the added touch she desired.

"Thank goodness for those pills. Damn, what happened to me?" she muttered, getting up and facing the mirror. Poking out her tongue, she noticed its grayish color. "Something's not right," she said, closing her mouth and staring at every angle of her face.

Her perfect bow lips stood out, and along with her straightened teeth and lively brown eyes, Carrie attracted many to her. But now, as she brushed her short hair, she tried to recall what she had eaten at dinner the night before. She questioned why she looked drawn. Underneath her eyes, a dark bluish color stared back. "What's the matter with me? I have these ugly bags under my eyes! I look like the lost weekend. Oh my God, did I get food poisoning? I'm so bloody ugly," she said, straightening up some green bath towels on a rack.

Looking over her newly dyed hair, she questioned if she should stay a blonde. Her natural hair was brown, but now the newer reds in salons and the pictures in television ads appealed, so she thought she might become a redhead.

Carrie considered some clothing styles she saw in magazines as obscure, and often said, "I wouldn't be caught dead in any of them." Nevertheless, like a chameleon, she constantly changed her apparel on a whim. When she did, she was met with glares from strangers who frowned and gave her a peculiar ugly look.

"I don't care what others say or think," she would often say. "And it seems everyone wants to blurt out something about me and my outfits. Is it so wrong to be different? I don't want to be a carbon copy of everybody else." Miniskirts of the 1970's were back in fashion, and she vowed never to wear one. She saw them as tasteless, and definitely not her style. She desired something else, something a little more daring, and that was a tattoo of a butterfly on her right leg or ankle; but promised her parents she would not mutilate her body. She had read that one might get an infection from needles if you got a tattoo, and it could cost as much as a computer.

Since she hadn't the funds, she decided to think about it. Besides, she had seen young adults covered with loads of monstrous tattoos. Nevertheless, she thought one small butterfly on her right ankle would be divine.

"I need to go out," she said, turning on the sink tap and splashing cold water on her face. "After all, it's Sunday, a day off and time for some fun."

Carrie thought the Skylight Inn was better than the picture postcard that Matilda had recently sent. It was there in that fabulous ballroom Mark and Matilda were married and she had been the only bridesmaid. After the wedding, Carrie extended her vacation. She indulged herself in viewing fountains and tropical flowers, two enormous pools, one inside and one out, with service that even royalty would envy. "I loved it in Miami Beach at Christmas when Matilda married Mark. Oh, for some real money. I just have to go back, but Matilda lives in Twinsburg and that's in Ohio, not gorgeous Miami Beach. Oh what can I say? Who knows if I'll ever get back to the Skylight Inn?"

At the wedding, Carrie had met Richard Evergreen along with his children, Joey and Jenny. Matilda had been a nanny to them and they loved her. Carrie saw Richard as a lonely widower, who she thought might want to get to know her. He was handsome with his slightly gray curly hair, hazel eyes, slim muscular build, and a smile similar to Paul Newman, the late actor, who Carrie had seen on the classic movie reruns on TV.

Richard's quiet manner suggested a mystery to her. After touring with him around Miami Beach, he had mentioned that he might visit London. She remembered him asking her to show him the tourists' sites if he came. Returning home, Carrie thought about Richard and expected a letter from him, but it never arrived, which surprised her. "It's Matilda he wanted all along I suppose," she said forlornly. "That's why he never came to London."

Leaving the bathroom, she approached her brown, upholstered armchair with broken springs and tried to get comfortable. Sitting there thinking, she curled up and rested her head on a pillow. Jolted out of her thoughts by the familiar sing-song-ring of the phone, she hurried to the kitchen counter. She picked up the phone.

"Hi, Carrie it's me, Shania. So what are you doing? We can't play tennis. Do you want to go out?"

Hearing Shania's voice, Carrie brightened up. "I sure do."

Shania, her new friend who she had met at the tennis club, had come from Jamaica to London with her parents when she was two years old. Shania Della, just nineteen had told Carrie she wanted to become a serious jazz artist. Shania had made a few demos of her husky singing voice and mailed them out to various nightclubs in London. Carrie had become impressed with Shania's voice and often encouraged her to keep working with her coach. Carrie had told Shania many times she was as good as Lena Horn, a great black singer of the Twentieth century.

"What do you want to do?" asked Shania, blinking her sensuous brown eyes adorned by thick lashes. "How about meeting me at Roebean's Coffee House around three? We can catch up, and you can tell me what's going on in your life?"

Carrie gave those words some thought. She knew this was a remark people said when greeting, but she seriously wondered where her future lay. Living in London with the cost of living high and a bad economy had her mind racing. She knew she needed to return to school and learn what ever was necessary to gain a better paying job. Most evenings she spent investigating employment opportunities advertised on the Internet and the daily London newspapers. She paused before she answered. "Oh, nothing much is happening," she said, gazing out of the window, but it'll be great going out Shania. See you soon at Roebean's."

Carrie headed to her bedroom. For late August it was a cool day; so out of her wardrobe she selected a blue plaid skirt, a white lace blouse, and her new high black boots. On her second finger on her right hand, she slipped on an opal ring. On her left hand she selected a sparkling ring for each finger. Handling the necklaces, bracelets, and broaches, she sat a while admiring them, fingering them, smiling, and trying them on. She had inherited the collection of costume jewelry from her great maternal grandmother who had been the most talked about member in the family.

Her great-grandmother, Josephine had lived in the 1920s, collected costume jewelry. In her youth, she spent time searching out a variety of gems. The jewelry she chose had been designed by famous artists of her day. Josephine was a flapper, who had worn slinky clothes, bobbed her hair, wore lots of makeup, smoked cigarettes without her father knowing, and danced at London nightclubs whenever she got the chance. She liked to dance the Charleston that had swept from America. Women practiced the moves until they got the dance right. When the First World War ended, Josephine with her young friends decided to have some fun after so many violent deaths of British and American soldiers.

Carrie embraced the stories of her great-grandmother handed down through her family, and often sat by her dresser turning the pages forward and backward of an old photograph album. She admired great-grandmother Josephine who draped herself in dazzling dresses. Carrie often said she would have liked to have worn any one of them. In the faded photos, Carrie tried to imagine what it was like living in her great-grandmother's time. She was told that Josephine had loads of admirers, both rich and poor. One was Carrie's great-grandfather, Alexander, debonair but with no money of his own who danced the tango and had slick black hair with the look of Rudolph Valentino, an actor who appeared in silent films of the nineteen twenties. Valentino had thousands of female fans sighing and fainting when he appeared in the public arena. Alexander imitated him, and it had been said he could excite the goddess Venus, for he, too, had his share of women admirers chasing after him. But it was Josephine he loved, so without a pause she married her knight.

In her later years, Carrie's great-grandmother often stated she should have married a rich man who would have given her anything she desired, but instead she had married for love. Bitterly, she complained to her family about not having enough money to purchase a house, which she wanted above anything else.

Carrie was told she resembled her great-grandmother in looks and personality. For one thing, she was independent, and unafraid to say what she thought about most things; so if anyone wanted the truth, it was best to stay away from Grandmother Josephine. Carrie held the framed photograph that sat on her dresser. The black and white picture showed Josephine in a slinky dress with a ruffle at the bottom. Her wavy short brown hair and her large brown eyes were lit up like fireflies. Carrie liked looking at the photograph which was in an old fashioned carved wood frame. Carrie put the picture back on her dresser next to a journal that she tried to write in twice a week. She opened her journal and wrote the date and entry: "Today, August the 24th, Anne Wiggins, who is now Mrs. Josh Smith, called to tell me Matilda is divorcing Mark Rosen." Carrie wrote another word, "Shocking!" Underneath the comment, she drew a curvy line.

Returning to the bathroom, she pasted her eyelashes with brown mascara and selected a commercial brand that made her eye lashes appear longer. Satisfied with her appearance, she left the bathroom. "I'm off, Pete," she called. Closing the front door, she opened up her green umbrella. The rain hadn't stopped. She liked it splashing on her face and coat collar. Striding over the puddles in her high-heeled shiny boots, she was careful not to get mud on them, and with her umbrella held high, she tiptoed to the bus stop. She couldn't wait to see Shania, for they liked to talk lots and laugh lots about anything they fancied.

Two

Anne's Thoughts

Anne Smith folded the evening newspaper and placed it on a shelf. Usually, she devoured the articles, but since Matilda's departure for Ohio, she couldn't concentrate. The change in her daughter's life nagged at her, and she felt caught in the middle of Matilda's dilemma.

Anne divorced when her children were young. Her husband had drunk his whisky every night, while she did her best to protect her children from his violent outbursts. She had pressed him to get some counseling, but he had refused. After her divorce, she lived as a single parent for eighteen years until Josh Smith entered her life, but it took lots of convincing for her to marry him. With Josh, she had found her life partner, and at fifty-two years of age, she had changed her life. Immersed in her memories, she looked up at the sound of the front door opening. Josh walked in. Nifty, their black and white cat, greeted him as he hung his raincoat in the closet.

"How are you, Nifty?" he said, picking him up and examining his half tail. "Have you stayed out of trouble today? We don't want you to lose the rest of that tail. No more accidents for you! You're the cat with nine lives. So where is my favorite wife?" Josh held the purring, family cat as he went to find Anne.

He put Nifty down. "We've been married a fortnight, and should begin planning that trip to Hawaii. It will be a great honeymoon for us. Don't you think? You, winning the best waitress award in London really is smashing."

"Oh, Josh, I haven't given it much thought. It's Matilda I'm thinking about. How's she going to make it on her own now she's separated from Mark Rosen? She's never mentioned how much money she saved for the university classes. And she's never asked for a penny. Eric paying for her trip here this summer was a Godsend. He's such a good son and so generous. It was wonderful seeing her. I've been thinking about the money I won, and I've made my decision. Some of it has to go to her."

"Really, if that's what you think is best. It's your money to do what ever you wish."

"Money, as I've said before isn't everything. Matilda married a rich man who she thought she loved. She was too young, but I'm lucky to have won that Best Waitress prize and the trip to Hawaii. I've never had much money and it doesn't matter a thing to me. If she needs help with her education, I'm ready to do that. I'm a lucky woman. But you're right, we have to decide on a date, or I might lose the trip. That part of my prize is just lovely."

"I'm ready whenever you are. Stop worrying about Matilda. She's an adult. She'll get her divorce and will marry Richard. Isn't that the plan?"

"I suppose it is, so it's bound to happen. When she was the children's nanny, she took good care of them and formed a loving attachment. She should have married Richard in the first place. Don't you think? I just don't know. I'm wondering if she'll continue on with her education. I so want her to finish. What can I say? Getting an education is important. But life is not a straight road. Is it?" said Anne, hugging him.

"Straight? No never. One never knows what's coming next even when one plans. Here is a little something for you." Josh thrust a small wrapped package into Anne's hand. Her eyes wore a curious glow. Opening the box, she discovered a fine gold chain necklace, with their initials and wedding date. Anne beamed while Josh slipped the necklace around her neck and fastened it.

"There, it looks nice. Wear it in good health."

In the hallway mirror, Anne gloated. It's smashing, Josh," she said, returning to the living room. "I'm one happy woman, and I'm no longer Anne Wiggins. I'm Mrs. Josh Smith, and I love the name and you. I should have married you a lot sooner. I suppose I was just scared to make the decision. I can't think why now. Thank you. I'll cherish it."

"That's good to hear." said Josh, kissing his new bride.

"I enjoy these three day weekends. It's like getting a mini vacation. Did you notice my feet? They look better since I'm not wearing high heels all day. Remember how you made me wear those nurses' shoes." Josh looked over Anne's bare feet and painted red toe nails.

"I like working at the Charlene Restaurant," said Anne, putting on a pair of socks.

Josh laughed. "Your feet look fine. They are pretty. As long as they don't hurt and there's no corns giving you pain. We'll be walking lots and viewing the sites, so don't take the high heels on our trip."

"I won't. September should be perfect. I love that month. Do you want to go then?"

"That'll be fine with me."

"Okay, I'll make the arrangements, but I'll have to leave Nifty at the vets. That's the only thing. I'll hate leaving him there. Last time I left him with Emily and look what happened? He had that awful accident and lost half his tail. I know it wasn't her fault, but my cat sitting in a cage for days bothers me. I don't think I can handle that."

"He'll be all right."

Anne sighed. "I'll have to decide what to do."

"Look, I have some brochures of Hawaii. I sent away for them.

There are ten big attractions. Most of all, we can pay our respects to Pearl Harbor and the American sailors who died there in the Second World War. Then we can check out Na Pali Coast, and see those waterfalls and tropical streams. There's so much beauty to be seen. We won't know what to do first. I'll call in the morning for some more information."

"Ooh, I can't believe we'll be staying in one of these five star hotels. I can't wait to go. Come on Nifty, let's get to the kitchen and get you fed."

In the kitchen, Anne switched on the radio. The news announcer talked of the government cutting back paychecks and jobs. "Those poor devils, what are they supposed to do? We have too many losing jobs. Our country is in a bloody mess. Everyday there's something else to worry about. I don't know what the world's coming to, and look at this weather! It's bloody awful. It's got to be all this Global warming that's causing us grief." Bending down, she stroked her cat. "You finished that lot fast, and now I suppose you'll want to prowl the neighborhood."

Josh who had changed into comfortable jeans came out of the bedroom. "I'll be watching some TV while you're cooking dinner. Do you want some help?"

"I'm fine, Josh."

In all her life, Anne had never had a summer like this. Winning the Best Waitress award, waiting on that famous actress Deanna Lockhart from the States, getting her autograph, marrying Josh Smith, and her Matilda coming from Miami Beach to their wedding was beyond heaven. Just thinking of all these events had her dancing around the kitchen. She turned up the radio dial and bounced to the beat of a popular song.

"What's going on in there? Am I missing something?" called Josh.

"No, love, everything is fine. I just like the song, so I'm having a go." She stopped dancing and rummaged in the kitchen cupboard. Finding a frying pan among the cluttered pots, she pulled it out and stuck it on the top of her cooker. The phone rang.

"Anne, it's for you. It's Carrie," called out Josh.

"Carrie? Tell her I'll give her a ring after supper."

"Will do," said Josh.

"Me marrying Josh has made life better," she said to herself as she cut up some onions. "Ouch, my eyes are tearing. It would be nice if onions didn't burn my eyes, but they make the food ever so tasty, so I have to put up with it." She pulled out a pair of sunglasses from a kitchen drawer and put them on. "That's better," she said, mixing up the onions.

Finishing up, she removed the sunglasses and pulled out a kitchen chair and sat down. Watching the pots bubbling up, she said, "There's nothing like a home cooked meal. Those fast food restaurants make such tasteless food and make you fat." Having watched the chefs cooking at the Charlene Restaurant, Anne managed to come up with some ideas to become a better cook.

"Come on, Josh, turn off the tube. Let's have dinner. Too bad we don't have some elegant candles to set off the table tonight. A little glamour makes things nice. Don't you think?"

"Who needs candles? Just looking at you is enough for me. Not only did I marry a beautiful woman, I've married an expert cook."

"You just better say that," said Anne, handing him a dinner plate.

Three

A Trauma

Brian Price sat at his desk checking the calendar dates to meet with clients. Recently promoted to advertising manager, he was immersed in photographs of fashion models. Selected pictures were to be placed in various London magazines advertising Yamzing's newest designs. On his schedule was the upcoming autumn show which was generally held at the company's large warehouse.

For three years Brian had tried for a promotion, but had lost to another candidate. Now he beamed. Ideas floating in his brain poured forth while he spun around in his swivel chair; he got up, paced around the office, and drank from his bottled water. He returned to his desk. "I can do this," he said. Having been chosen from the many applicants who had applied for the position, he wanted to do his best. His eyes wandered over his desk scattered with notebooks. He often took one with him and jotted down ideas when he saw something he thought would be useful.

His eyes gleamed, and his hair was brushed into a neat style. Removing his pin stripped jacket, he rolled up his sleeves, loosened his Mickey Mouse tie and began making phone calls to clients. It was an hour before he finished. On his desk sat his new phone. For few minutes, he practiced familiarizing himself with its different programs.

Often, he heard his mother say, "Why do we need all this new fangled stuff? Don't we have enough? If I had pots of money, I'd buy my own island like some of those American movie stars and get some peace. How much technology do we need? It's taken away our privacy. It's not for me."

"This is how the world works, Mum. Change is how it is. You have to try to adjust," he would tell her.

Closing a folder, he checked his watch and pulled out another file. Miss Sabrina Zack, the office assistant, was expected any moment to discuss plans and brainstorm ideas for the week. Picking up his ringing phone, he heard a familiar voice.

"Hello, Brian. Congratulations on your promotion at Yamzing's. How you doing? Is everything going okay? So, what time do you plan to eat lunch today? Are we going to that new Irish pub overlooking the river bank? I've heard their sandwiches are spectacular, so it might be hard to get a table."

"Go to lunch? Where did my morning go? Are you still angry with me?"

"Angry? Someone had to get the job. My interview with the big man was bad. I can still see Mr. Bloom's eyes penetrating me. I remember you telling me they wanted a man for the position, and that part did make me want to scream, and I did that at home. I suppose my one year at business school is not enough. I need more courses."

Brian swallowed. "Carrie, that's a good thing for you to do, but I can't make it for lunch today. My assistant is bringing me a sandwich. I'm on overload with the new autumn season coming upon us, but I'll miss you. Tomorrow should be better."

"Oh, that's a shame. Okay, tomorrow then."

Carrie had appreciated Brian helping her when she began her job. Their friendship was important to her. They often went to lunch together, but now she wondered if he'd ever make it out of his office. He had helped her through some mixed up documents, which almost made her flip out and return to biting her fingernails, which were now long and painted with her favorite nail varnish. She was pleased she had kicked that habit.

Picking up her small purple leather shoulder bag, she searched for her cologne, then sprayed a little on her wrists. After touching up her makeup, she decided to get something to eat. Not eating much at breakfast, her stomach started growling. Reaching the cafeteria, Carrie located one empty seat by a long table filled with men. Looking around, she noticed many of the supervisors and her immediate boss, Mr. Frank Evans, eating. She stood up to leave the table. Frank looked up, brushed his jet black hair over his forehead, grinned, and with a wave of his hand welcomed her.

"Hello, Carrie, don't leave. It'll be nice to have you join us for lunch. Gentlemen, this is Carrie Adler. She works in my department."

Pushing the chair forward, she turned around. "Oh, I just want a little something. I'm not that hungry for a big lunch," said Carrie, knowing she lied. "I'll take something back to the office. Nice to meet you all," she said, stepping away from the table.

"So that's the new girl," said one man. "She's good to look at."

"She is," said Mr. Evans, "but most of all she's doing good work."

Carrie joined the cafeteria line and decided on the casserole, dessert, and a cup of coffee. Clearing the important documents away from her desk, she began eating, but suddenly stopped. She didn't feel right, and couldn't grasp what was wrong. She felt a slight pain in her stomach and couldn't eat. Cleaning up the desk, she put her meal aside and wiped her mouth with a paper napkin. The staff began returning along with Frank Evans who approached her.

"Hello, Carrie. You didn't have to leave us. Our conversation at lunch can be very dull. You should have stayed and brightened things up. How long have you been with us?"

"A little over three months," answered Carrie, a little startled.

"You're doing fine. Do you have any questions that need answering?"

"I don't believe so. I'll have the papers ready for you by the end of the day."

"Good, okay," said Frank raising an eyebrow and smoothing down his hair. He smiled at her and left.

Carrie pulled out the mirror she had tucked in her desk drawer and gave her hair a quick comb. She felt pleased with herself. "I knew I was doing all right in this job," she said to herself. Putting back the mirror, she felt the sharp pain again, grinding in her abdomen and on the side of her stomach. "Oh, dear God, the pain is back," she moaned holding her stomach and rolling from side to side. Throwing up and soiling the important documents, she shook, unable to control her body. "Please, please help me!" she cried out. Crouching over, limp, with her head on the desk, she lost her grip and fell to the floor.

Across the aisle, a woman engrossed in her computer, heard Carrie's scream and rushed to her. She knelt down and comforted her and then phoned 999. Soon the office was full of people running and trying to help.

"Get out of the way all of you," yelled Frank. He held Carrie's hand and stroked her forehead. "You'll be all right," he said in a whisper.

Within five minutes an ambulance arrived, and Carrie was placed on a stretcher by paramedics. Frank joined Carrie in the ambulance while a paramedic took her blood pressure.

Arriving at the hospital, Carrie was examined by an emergency room doctor. Evaluating her, he saw her condition as serious; a surgeon was paged. It was determined she had appendicitis and sent immediately to surgery.

Frank Evans sank into a chair in the waiting room, trying to think what to do next. Glancing at a magazine, he flipped through some pages and looked up to see a hospital volunteer.

"Hello there, I'm Lucy. Can I get you something? How about a nice hot cup of strong tea and a bun?" she asked in a cheerful voice. "I saw you come in. You look as though you could use some refreshment."

"Thanks, that would be nice," he said.

Lucy took off and returned quickly with steaming tea and a bun, which she handed to Frank.

"Thank you, you've been most kind. It's just what I needed," said Frank, hitting the buttons on his phone. His secretary answered.

"Hello, Ruby, please look up Carrie Adler's parents' number and tell them their daughter is in the hospital, and that I'm with her," said Frank in a tired voice.

"Certainly, Mr. Evans, I'll do that right away."

"Thanks, Ruby."

Four

The Waiting

Gary and Rita Adler sat with Frank Evans in the hospital waiting room. They had driven two hours from their home. Frank explained what had happened to their daughter.

"Oh my Lord," said Rita. "I had no idea."

"Mr. Evans, I appreciate you getting Carrie to the hospital," said Gary, shaking Frank's hand. "I can't thank you enough. It was lucky you were there. I need to find a nurse and see what's going on." He took off down the corridor to the nurses' station.

Frank turned to face Rita "Can I get you something to eat?"

"No thank you."

"You've had quite a trip," said Frank. "The surgery should be over soon. I've been staring at my watch, counting how long she's been in there," he said, glancing down the hallway at Gary.

"You don't have to stay. We'll be okay. I'm sure you're a very busy man," said Rita with a worried look.

"Busy? I suppose I am, but I want to stay until Carrie's out of surgery."

"That's good of you," answered Rita.

Gary returned. "Rita, she's okay. She'll be in the recovery room soon. According to the doctor, she's lucky. It was a case of getting her to the hospital promptly," he said, looking at Frank Evans.

"That's good news," said Frank. I'll be on my way then. I wish Carrie a good recovery. Tell her not to worry about her job. We'll see her when she's better and ready to return to work."

"Mr. Evans, thank you so much," said Rita, watching him leave.

"What a kind man he is," said Rita, feeling relieved.

"He is," said Gary. "Let's find the recovery room. We'll ask the nurse at the desk when we can speak to her surgeon. Oh, look, that must be him!" said Gary as he saw a man with short gray hair dressed in surgical garb coming toward them. He held a folded newspaper and hit it on chairs as he came closer to them. Throwing the newspaper on a table, he came toward the Adler's.

Smiling, the surgeon greeted them. "Hello, Mr. and Mrs. Adler, I presume," said Doctor Hough.

"Yes, that's right," said Rita.

"Your daughter, Carrie, is fine. She has had an emergency appendectomy, but it would have been easier on her had she visited a doctor a lot sooner. She must have suffered a good amount of pain, which it seems she chose to ignore. Her surgery was a laparoscopic procedure which is using a video camera to view the abdominal cavity where we could locate her appendix. She'll sleep for twelve hours, and after that, we'll have her up and walking." He paused. "Do you have any questions?"

"Yes. I do. How long will it take her to fully recover?" asked Rita.

"I'd say around three to six weeks. She'll be able to go home in three days. She's on an antibiotic now."

"Thank you so much for everything you have done," said Rita. Doctor Hough smiled, shook their hands and left.

"Well, that's a relief," said Gary. "Come on. Let's ask the nurse at the desk where the recovery room is. We can wait for her there."

"What a nightmare," said Rita, holding her coat. "I feel so drained."

"Come on, you don't have to worry now; she's going to be okay."

"I hope you're right. What would have happened to her if she hadn't been at work when she collapsed?" said Rita, opening up the door to the recovery room. "I can't make my mind think of that. I've never liked her living on her own, but she wanted her independence. You know, no one can be completely independent, but you can't tell Carrie that."

Opening the door, they observed a nurse working on a computer near the bedside.

"Hello, we're Carrie's parents."

"Nice to meet you. Carrie's sleeping off the anesthetic. I'll be here most of the time, so if you'd like something to eat, there's a snack bar not far from the main lobby. It has a good variety of sandwiches. I'm Ellen."

"Sounds good."

"We have to have someone look after Oscar. Alice Shelton has the key to let him out. Damn, I almost forgot about the dog."

"I'll ring her up now," said Gary, going to the door.

Rita recalled Carrie bringing Oscar to stay with them. Carrie did not have a big enough flat to keep him, and he needed to run and exercise, so she had decided it would be better for her dog to stay with her parents. Rita grew attached to him, and it looked like Oscar was hers now.

"There's a cot bed I can bring in if you'd like to rest," said Ellen.

"That would be so nice," said Rita, yawning. "I'm exhausted."

"I can see that. I'll be back in a minute."

Gary returned to find Rita sleeping and the nurse gone. "Well, I'll be darned," he said, sitting down. He held the evening newspaper and flipped through it. "Rita's all in. Looks like I'm in for a long night," he mumbled. He put the newspaper aside, got up and gently clasped his daughter's hand and whispered, "Sorry, Carrie, wish I had known."

Five

Getting Well

Carrie awakened to see her father sitting in the chair. "Dad, what happened to me?" she asked.

"Hold on. Don't move. You had surgery. You're in a London Hospital."

"What?"

The door opened and a nurse entered. Rita stood by Carrie's bed.

"Okay, you two can take off for breakfast. Carrie will be getting a sponge bath," said the nurse.

"Mom, wait, come back here," called Carrie in a weak voice.

Rita turned around. "We'll see you in a little bit, dear," she said, closing the door.

"What surgery did I have?" Carrie asked.

"You were brought here by ambulance yesterday with a ruptured appendix which could have led to an infection. You're a lucky young lady, so smile. Be glad it's all over. Let's get you freshened up!" said the nurse.

"Oh, my God, I had that rotten pain at work. I couldn't move," said Carrie, pulling the sheet over her head. "Oh, I can't face anyone at Yamzing's ever again."

The nurse pulled back the top sheet. "Come on, Carrie, it will be all right. Sometimes things happen that we have no control of. Here, take this pill. After breakfast, we'll get you walking down the corridor. Your breakfast will be here any minute." She dropped a flannel in a warm bowl of water. "Here, you'll feel better after you wash your face."

"Breakfast, what am I getting?"

"Yogurt."

"I don't want it. I'd like a cream cheese bagel."

"There'll be no bagels for three weeks or longer! It'll be yogurt today, apple sauce, and some broth later on. You have to heal."

"You're tough," moaned Carrie.

Entering with a tray, an older woman from the dietary staff brought in a dish of yogurt. She set the tray by Carrie.

"Here you are my dear," said the woman.

Carrie wrinkled up her nose and frowned. "Thank you," she said, and pushed the tray aside.

"I'm off," said the nurse. "Press the bell by your bed if you should need anything. Eat up. In an hour a therapist will be coming to get you walking, and in three days you'll be going home. You should be off to a shared room sometime today."

Looking at the pale green walls, Carrie sighed. She pulled herself up and felt a twinge in her stomach. Feeling hungry, she took a bite of yogurt and then another until she scraped the last morsel from the bowl. She recalled visiting others in the hospital and seeing some older patients sleeping with their mouths open and drugged, but could never have imagined herself being a patient. During the night, she had heard the patter of quick footsteps of nurses up and down the hallway, and doors opening and closing.

"No rest here," she had thought. "I'm a fumbling idiot, a spectacle to be talked about. I can never go back to Yamzing's. No way," she said out loud, "Never!" Visions of curious faces, whisperings, and wanting to know why she had fallen, had her pulling the top sheet up to cover her face. "Hell, I can't ever face them. I can't ever go back there!"

A light tap on the door stirred her. Her parents opened the door.

"How you doing?" asked her mother "Did you eat?"

"Yes, I did. Looks like I'll move to a room sometime today."

"That's good. I'm going to your flat and see how Pete is doing. Dad will stay with you. We'll be sleeping at your flat until you're released," said her mother. "Okay, dear?"

Carrie turned her face toward the pillow attempting to hide her tears, and then looked at her mother. Rita kissed her daughter on the forehead. "Bye love. I'll let you know how Pete is doing. I'm sure he's hungry. Chin up dear, you'll be fine."

"Mom, what about Oscar? Who's caring for him?"

"Not to worry, we are lucky. Our neighbor is helping us. We've worked out everything. When you come down to the country, you'll see your terrier, and you'll get better there."

Carrie lay back. She stared at her mother's expression and then at her father who sat with his legs outstretched and his head buried in the newspaper.

"Thanks, Mom, for everything," said Carrie in a soft voice.

Rita Adler smiled and gripped her daughter's hand. "I'll be back soon," she said, closing the door.

Gary put the newspaper down. "We have to get you up and about soon. I checked the front desk, and I've been told they're getting you out of that bed any minute."

"Dad, how can they do that? I'm tired. I don't feel like moving at all."

"That's the order. Don't you want to get on the back of my motor bike and fly around the countryside? Helen of Troy awaits you!"

"Oh, dad, I just love the name you gave your bike," she said, laughing. "Oh, it hurts when I laugh."

"All right, that's enough of my big mouth."

The door opened. "Carrie Adler?" asked a young man holding a clipboard with information on Carrie.

"Yes, that's me."

"Okay, it's time to take you dancing down that corridor. I just have to check your wrist for the right name. Ready?"

"Oh, no, not really," said Carrie as the physical therapist checked her hospital bracelet.

"Not to worry. I'm really Superman in disguise. I'm here to catch you should you decide to trip over my ankle."

"In that case, I'm ready," said Carrie.

Six

The Message

"All right I'm coming," yelled Anne to the ringing phone. "Josh where are you? Oh, you're playing that Patience card game. Damn, I'll have to answer it. I can't get used to that bloody thing. Oh well, here goes. The dinner is in the cooker, Josh. Okay, watch it please. "Good evening, Anne speaking," she said, almost stuttering.

"Hello, Anne, this is Rita Adler. How are you? Carrie gave us your phone number. I'm calling to let you know she's in the hospital."

"What? I just spoke to her the other day. She never said a word that she wasn't feeling well. Oh, I'm so sorry."

"She had her appendix out. She's doing okay. She did say she wants to see you."

"She had her appendix out? Really, that's a shock! When can I go and visit?"

"Can you see her tomorrow?"

"I think so. I'll try and leave work early. Thank you for calling me. Tell her I'll be there." Anne hung up the phone and called out to Josh who was still immersed in his Patience card game. He removed his glasses and blankly looked up. "What's going on?"

"Josh, Rita Adler, Carrie's mother just phoned. You won't believe this but our Carrie is in the hospital."

He raised his eyebrows. "What's she doing there?" he asked, looking as though he had been struck by a brick.

"She's had her appendix out."

"Blimey, when did that happen? Is she all right?"

"She had the surgery yesterday, and according to her mother, she's recovering just fine."

"That's good, but what a shame to have to go through that!"

"It is. I told Carrie about Matilda last Sunday, but she didn't say much. I'm sure she was surprised. I never did get a chance to tell her the details. She hung up pretty quick. I just said she was separating from Mark. At the time, she never mentioned one word about any pain she was having. I'll ring her now, and let her know I'll see her soon."

"Do you want me to go with you?"

"Nah, if she's up to it, we'll just gab. Besides, you said you have to work overtime tomorrow night."

"That's right, I do."

"Then that's settled. Here goes, I have to ring her at the hospital. I still don't want to use the bloody phone. I hope I'll dial the right number."

"You're getting better at it. The more you use it, the more comfortable you'll get. There has to be a reason why you have a problem talking on the phone."

"I think I know, Josh. I didn't get a message right or something when I was a kid. My mother blew up and said I was stupid for not paying attention. Her face was cherry red. She pulled the phone from me and slammed it down. She then called back to whoever it was and apologized. I don't know if that's the reason for sure. I can't seem to make small talk. There's this waitress at work; she talks on the phone for hours. The boss can't get a message to her. Why does she do that? What can she say that takes so bloody long?"

"In that case, you're right. Some people are addicted to the phone and whatever's next on the social media, but answering the phone is important. Don't you think?"

"I know it is. Now it's all the other gimmicks we have today I don't like. The new technology confuses me, too. I feel lost. Okay, I'll give Carrie a call."

"Good idea."

After speaking to Carrie, Anne picked up Nifty and hugged him. "Carrie asked about your escapades, Nifty. I told her you're just full of it as usual."

"See, you did fine handling the phone, so what did you find out?" asked Josh, collecting up his cards and placing them in a box.

"Oh, she's in a room with two other patients, and one is groaning something awful. Carrie wants ear plugs. Nope, she's not happy in that room, but she squealed when she heard my voice. I'll get over there as soon as I can. I better send a quick note to Matilda. She'd want to know about her friend. I'll get it off tomorrow. In this world, you never bloody know what's going to happen next! Don't let me forget to post it in the morning."

"I'll remind you. I've made some phone calls for our pending trip to Hawaii."

"That's super, Josh."

"I'm working on the best deal. In a couple of days I should have it all settled."

"Josh, that's just lovely." Anne beamed at Nifty who had climbed up on the armchair and curled up next to her. "Nifty," she said. "I need to relax. I think I'll take a warm bath and use that heavenly lavender soap. Josh, please continue to watch the cooker. I'm going for a soak. We can eat later."

"That's fine," said Josh.

Seven

Shania Della

Shania Della placed her handbag behind the reception desk in the beauty salon. She picked up the appointment book. In August, many of her clients went away on holiday, so she did not expect too many to come in. She ran her index finger down the telephone numbers of her regular clients. Picking up a 1930's elegant antique telephone, she dialed each number to confirm the appointments for the day. When she completed the list, she called Carrie's number.

"Maybe she visited her parents," she said to herself. Discouraged at not reaching her friend, she tried Carrie's office phone number.

"This is Yamzing's," the female voice answered. "How may I direct your call?"

"I think I want the Quality Control Department," said Shania.

"Fine, I'll connect you."

"Hello, Frank Evans speaking."

"Is this the Quality Control Department?" asked Shania.

"Yes, how can I help you?"

"I'd like to speak with Carrie Adler."

"Who's calling?"

"Oh, I'm Shania Della, a friend of hers. Is she there?"

"No, she isn't here today. She's recovering from recent surgery, but I believe she'll be leaving the hospital tomorrow."

"The hospital? How can that be? So that's why I haven't heard from her. Oh my goodness, what happened to her?"

"I can't say, but I'm sure she'll tell you. When you do reach her, tell her I send my best wishes for her recovery."

"What's your name again?"

"I'm Frank Evans, the director. Don't worry, from what I've learned, she's going to be fine."

"She is? That's good. Thank you."

Shania hung up the phone and watched a beautician working on an elderly lady having her white hair set. She approached the busy beautician.

"Oh, dear," she said. "I forgot to ask what hospital my friend Carrie is in. We were at a café a couple of days ago. Come to think of it, when I saw her there, I thought she seemed tired, definitely not her usual self. I don't even know what surgery she had," she said, speaking in a loud voice. "I'll have to call back later today to locate the hospital she's in."

"That's the best thing to do," said the beautician.

Gathering the used towels, Shania dropped them in a hamper in the backroom. Locating a broom, she swept out hair from under the beautician's chairs, and cleaned the mirrors to a polished shine. Recently, Shania had earned a certificate as a manicurist and expected a client any minute.

On Shania's mind now was the Palm Jazz Club. She had signed a contract to sing there and had been anxious to share this big news with Carrie. Before the audition, she had sung her songs to her mother. Singing in front of her mother gave her confidence, but not when singing to other family members.

In an interview, Shania had convinced the manager of the club to let her sing for no payment the first week, and had noticed his eyes glitter when she sang an old classic of Louie Armstrong.

Her parents had played jazz and the standards on the stereo when she was young, so the imprint of this music dwelled within her. She dreamed of a future career as a singer, and while selecting nail varnishes for her clients, she often imagined becoming a great singer like Pearl Bailey. Standing by her chair, she looked at the glass door and waited for her client. The door opened and in came a middle-aged woman.

"Hello ducky," said the woman with long faded blond hair. "My nails look horrible. I forgot to put on my rubber gloves when I did the dishes last night. I was just so tired when I got to them that I broke a nail while scrubbing my steel pots last night. They're an awful mess, they are, and I've a wedding to attend to next Saturday. I'd like my hands to look fabulous. You'll have a job fixing that nail. Do you suppose you have a color to match a special dress?"

"What color is it?"

The woman laughed. "I was going to wear my red one, but my derrière seems to have blossomed lately, so I'll have to wear my black dress after all. I can't seem to stay out of the biscuit box."

"Mrs. Landis, you can choose any color then."

"Let me think a minute. I know. I'll go with that new peach that's just come out."

"Sounds right, let's go with that. It'll make a nice change for you. Let me take care of that nail."

"Oh, it's so good to relax. In my house, I can't seem to ever get done. Tell me what's happening with your singing. Have you got a gig yet?"

"I have, would you like to come and see me?" she asked, varnishing Mrs. Landis's nails.

"Of course I would. Just write the date down for me and I'll be there."

"I'll do that before you leave. I suppose I admire most that new jazz singer, Esperanza Spalding. She's getting a lot of attention, and I want to be as good as her, but it's the other singers that seem to have made it big. Take Lady Gaga, Justin Bieber, Taylor Swift, Lil Wayne, and Kate Perry. What a career they've made for themselves, and they are so young!"

"I don't care for their stuff. There must be something wrong with my ears because I know how popular they are, or maybe it's my age. I like jazz. It's been around a long time, and most of the young people haven't listened to it, which is a real shame. I'm surprised that you being so young would sing the old stuff. I think jazz began in the 1920s, or it could be earlier. You might like to come over sometime and listen to my records I've collected. I still have an old record player that works."

"I'd like that. Okay, I've just your little finger left and you'll be all set. How do you like the shade?"

"It looks okay. I suppose it makes a change for me from those reds I've been using. It's sort of posh."

"Who's getting married?"

"My husband's partner at the fire station has finally decided to get married."

"That's nice. Have fun."

"I plan to. Weddings are lovely. It's the funerals I hate," said Mrs. Landis. She paid the bill and made another appointment.

"See you soon," said Shania, opening the door for her client.

"How's everything going?" called out one of the hair dressers.

"Fine," answered Shania.

"Could you take care of my customer and set up the hair dryer for her? I have to make a quick phone call."

"Will do," answered Shania.

"Thanks, I won't be long."

Shania set the hair dryer to a comfortable range. The client smiled and opened up a magazine. Returning to the desk, Shania checked her appointment book. She didn't have a long wait. A high school girl came in chewing gum and wearing a smile as big as an orange.

    "Hi Shania," she said. "I just can't wait to get my nails done."

    "Then you're in the right place," laughed Shania.

    "Yeah, and I know the color I want."

    "You do? What shade will that be?" asked a smiling Shania."

    "I want different colors on each nail."

    Okay, what colors do you want?"

    "Pink, green, red, and black should do it."

    "Fine, I'll do that."

Eight

The Addition

The Skylight Inn in Miami Beach bustled with curious visitors, tourists, and the locals who had come to the opening of the new addition. Its pink stucco siding and green roof and black shutters gleamed under the evening sun. Attached to the new section was a restaurant designed for casual to formal celebrations, including a large parquet dance floor. In the foyer, an imported crystal light from France hung from the ceiling, along with modern paintings and a photograph of Sarah Evergreen, Richard's late wife. A sign hung above the door read "Sarah's Garden." Ron and Janet Rosen had spent months planning this opening. It was a dedication to honor their beloved dead daughter. They had examined every detail of the restaurant, and were pleased with the final touches. Tonight, they were ready to celebrate the opening of the extended wing. Ron and Janet Rosen had purchased the land thirty years earlier with the idea they would eventually build onto the Skylight Inn.

A long line formed early. All tickets had been sold, and the crowds were anxious to welcome the famous rock star, Bill Jenkins, who had flown from London to perform. He had sold millions of records, and considered the golden boy of England who had become an international star.

Ron Rosen in his stiff black tuxedo managed to smile. Janet wore chandelier earrings and a royal blue gown of silk organza, created by a famous designer. Janet chose her clothes well and elegancy was written all over her attire. Her eyes darted back and forth toward the door; she broke into a smile as she watched Mark enter. He strolled around the area, and then approached his father and hugged him.

"Well, dad, we made it. It's been hard work, but we can be proud of the results. I've never seen so many people come to our hotel. We should have hired Mr. Jenkins for the week."

"He couldn't do it. He has bookings all over the country, so we have to be grateful we have him first," said Ron Rosen.

"Right, Dad, we do. Come on, let's find our seats."

The door opened and the crowd poured in. An air of anticipation filtered through the area. The band warmed up and played the rock star's number one hit. A roar exploded when Bill Jenkins came out. Dressed in a white suit and a blue open shirt that showed of his muscular chest and broad shoulders, he bowed to the audience. His long blond hair was shoulder length and curled along his back. Lights dimmed and a spotlight zoomed on his face. The crowd screamed, and Bill sang, wowing the audience with his famous rock song. Singing an hour, he followed his performance with encores, for the audience would not let him leave. Finally, it was over. Bill Jenkins left his audience blowing kisses. Before leaving, he picked up the pink carnations scattered around him by his arduous fans.

"Well, they certainly got their money's worth," said Janet. "I'd say it was a hit."

"Can't argue with that," said Ron. "Come on. Let's see that he has everything he needs. We have invited a few fans to meet him. Those are the ones that bought the first tickets all those months ago. The photographer will be waiting to take their picture and ours."

"Right," said Mark and the three of them left to meet Bill Jenkins.

Flashbulbs and bright lights glared. Bill Jenkins stood next to the chosen fans who gathered to meet him. He smiled into the camera. Then they entered another room to meet the press, and the fans were given ample time to ask questions.

Meanwhile, Janet Rosen focused on her son. With the months of preparation over, she wanted to climb in bed and sleep and forget all that had happened this past year. She never approved of Matilda, and felt all along that Matilda was not right for Mark She could not understand why he had married a girl from such a dreadful family, a family she had decided had no education or status. Secretly, she was pleased that the upcoming divorce would free Mark. As for Mark, he had hardly acknowledged his mother since he announced that Matilda was divorcing him. He blamed her. This, Janet knew. Mark had told his mother she had interfered in his marriage and had belittled Matilda too many times. The coldness and animosity between them remained, so Mark had stated he would resign after the opening of the new addition. Would he really go? Janet had asked herself this question a million times.

The Skylight Inn was run mostly by Mark. Her two other sons, Aaron and Jay, were getting better at what was required to keep the hotel thriving, but Jay, just back after disappearing for months, remained a question mark. Would he return to gambling? His weekly therapy with the psychologist seemed to be going well. But what about Aaron? He was too young for full responsibilities. No, she could not let her beloved son leave. She had to make him stay. Lost in her thoughts, she did not hear what Ron was saying.

"Janet, are you listening? Mark has said the new addition is filled up for the month. Our customers will be coming from all over the world. What could be better?" said Ron. "We have honored our daughter. The sign at the entrance stands out, and her paintings give it class. I'll miss her forever," said Ron, placing a hand over his eyes, but the tears he tried to stop streamed down his rugged cheeks.

Janet took her husband's arm. "Come on, Ron, let's go back to the house, sit on the porch, relax, and listen to the ocean. I can think of no better sound. You know how much you enjoy that. You need to take it easy for a bit. We both do. We've accomplished our dream. Tomorrow you'll be so busy."

Janet chose her favorite deck chair and stretched out. She gazed up at the stars. Like many others, she wondered if there were other worlds out there in space. In the past, stars were described in magical terms, something a poet would write about for lovers and dreamers. Now the stars had new meanings, and new beginnings for man to discover. These distant lights calmed her, and she no longer wanted to recall the past. She turned to face the Skylight Inn and the new extension. Pride beamed on her face. She was glad their house had been built next to the hotel. Having it close proved convenient and easier to get to the hotel.

Their large porch at the back of the house filled with a variety of plants and comfortable outdoor furniture welcomed them. Early morning, they could catch the wild birds perched on the rocks. The porch had become a sanctuary, but since the death of Sarah, Janet had forced herself to keep herself occupied at The Rose restaurant, and to keep her mind filled, and not think of Sarah; so it was on a rare occasion she could enjoy the ocean.

Janet often visited the rabbi after the death of Sarah. It was he who had consoled her, so on this important day, the opening of the new addition, she remained calm. Looking over at Ron, she felt an inner peace. He pulled out his cigar and raised his eyebrows, waiting for her comments, and expecting her to utter a nasty remark about his smoking habit; but this time Janet simply smiled. He placed the cigar in his mouth, but did not light it.

"Can I get you something, dear?"

"Yep, a soda with lots of ice would be good."

"Okay, I'll be right back." Returning, she hesitated while watching her husband light up the Cuban cigar she knew he would never give up. Hating the odor, she entered the house to pour a drink. This evening, she had no desire to battle over his bad habit. This evening, she emptied her mind. This evening, she would not argue over the health issues of smoking.

She handed Ron his drink. "Here, I've put in plenty of ice. It's just the way you like it."

"Thank you dear," said Ron.

Nine

Returning Home

Carrie approached her terrier. "Come here, Oscar. Have you missed me? It's almost the end of August. I've been away from you too long." With that remark, her dog jumped on her lap and reached up to her face and smothered her with sticky licks. "Hey, that's enough." She put him down. "You're looking just fine. Mum is taking good care of you," she said, curling up on the sofa.

After much persuasion, Carrie had come home to recuperate. She thought she could manage her recovery but hadn't the strength to do much. Leaving London had not been in her plans. Her father had come up to check on her, and told her to pack her case after deciding she looked like a sad, sick cat.

"Look at you, you can barely walk around. It's time to come home and get well. We've painted the spare room green. I know you like that color. You had that shade in your bedroom in London. You never wanted to change it. Remember? Come on. I'll get Pete's food. He might like looking out the kitchen window at the garden. Throw some clothes in your suitcase and let's get out of here."

Carrie had hesitated. Her father had always been attentive to her, and rarely raised his voice, but this time he did. But the big disagreements had been with her mother, mostly over her choice of friends and the array of clothes scattered on the floor in her bedroom. Her teenage years had been emotional, and she often hid in her bedroom and locked her door and sobbed.

Her mother often said, "Carrie, you don't appreciate what you have. Children are starving in Africa. Your friend Matilda, has barely anything, and never complains. All you do is whine away and demand more." When she was fifteen, Carrie had nagged for a leather jacket. Her argument was, "All my friends have one."

Looking at her father, and the concern in his eyes, she had relented. She knew she needed to go home to get well. "Okay, Dad," she had said in almost a whisper. "I do love green rooms; they seem to have a healing effect."

Although Carrie did not want to live in the countryside, she had to admit the shady trees with their long branches, thick with leaves, surrounding her parents' country house, gave it an inviting, restful look. Her parents liked the red brick house with the white shutters. It was a welcoming sight. The rooms were painted with bright colors, giving those who visited a feeling of warmth. In contrast, Carrie could barely move in her tiny kitchen and often bumped into a cupboard door when not thinking to be careful.

Arriving at her parents' house, she had put Pete's cage on the sideboard. "You okay, Pete? You can look out the window in this house," she had said, and told her mother how peaceful the house looked and complained how much her rent was.

"I know," said Rita. "London is still for those with a top income and the very rich. How are you feeling? Your surgery was serious. You are fortunate to have gotten to the hospital in time. That kind manager of yours got you there We're so grateful.. Do you realize he saved your life?"

"I know, Mum. He's a good man, and I hardly know him. I don't want to talk about what happened to me. It's too embarrassing. Instead of going back to work, I wish I could go to Miami Beach and soak up the sun for a couple of weeks. One of these days I'll go back there and eventually travel the world."

"Are you serious?"

Carrie smiled. "I'll marry a wealthy man."

"That'll be good, but marriage? You never mentioned that before."

"My birthday's coming up. I'm the Halloween baby. What a crazy day for me to be born."

"Yes, it was. I was bombarded with cards with your arrival, and there were lots of jokes. You were such a big event, and I can't believe you're going to be twenty-one this year."

"No wonder I'm odd, Mum, and I'm getting old. I'm just thinking it might not be so bad to get married. Don't look so worried! I'm just thinking. Oh, forget what I just said. I have too many things I want to do. No one should marry until their twenty-eight years old. I think that's a decent age. Don't you? Oh, I don't know; I might just be single forever. Think of it, most don't get married these days, and marriage after a while must be so boring. How can anyone live with the same person forever?"

"Oh, my, Carrie, you never stop surprising me."

"It's Matilda that believes in marriage."

"Why do you say that?"

"I'm saying that because she's getting a divorce and, of all things, is planning to marry Richard Evergreen. Matilda's mother phoned to give me the news a few days ago. I have to get used to that, and I have to remember Anne's new last name. It's Smith now. I just want to say Mrs. Wiggins. That name suits her so well, but I don't understand Matilda anymore."

Rita opened her mouth and then closed it. "My God, when did all this happen?"

"Mum, I'm feeling tired. I'll tell you what I know later."

"Okay, just rest. I think I could do with a cup of tea." Quickly, Rita filled the kettle with cold water and waited for it to boil. She

43

selected her favorite brand of tea and then called out to her husband. Carrie left and went to the bedroom to rest.

"Gary, come join me for a cup of tea. We have to talk."

He came and sat down in the kitchen. "It's good thing that I brought her home. What's going on?"

"It's what your daughter just said. Here's your tea. Want a couple of biscuits?"

"You baked?"

"Yes. I made Carrie's favorites, but I forgot she can't eat any of them. She's on that soft diet."

"Is there something wrong?"

"No. Carrie just baffled me."

"What did she say?"

"She said Matilda is getting a divorce."

"Is that so?"

"It is."

"She just got married. How long did it last? It's just over a year. Isn't it? Well, I suppose that's her business."

"Gary, how can you talk that way?"

"Well, what can I say? Isn't that what goes on these days? I suppose it's the women's liberation thing. Most couples move in together and don't bother getting married. Isn't that so?"

"It seems it is," said Rita, dipping her biscuit into her tea. "But I can't understand any of the things that happen today. I'm not good at all the fast changes we have these days."

Ten

A Secret

Shania wrote out the phone number of Carrie's parents given to her by Frank Evans. Shania had tried to reach Carrie but had no luck. Most evenings Shania had been preparing for her singing debut. It was around supper time when she dialed the number given her.

"Hello, Gary speaking. Who's calling?"

"I'm Shania, a friend of Carrie's. Can she talk?"

"Certainly, as long as you like motorbikes," joked Gary, handing the phone to his daughter.

"Hello," said Carrie, wondering who it could be.

"Hello. It's me, Shania. How are you? I've been trying to reach you. Your boss told me you had surgery. He gave me your parents' phone number."

"He did? Oh, it's all so embarrassing. I collapsed at work. I had a rotten pain last Sunday, and I really shouldn't have gone out, but I thought it was just something I ate. I was over it when you called to go out. I'm getting better. I'll be staying with my parents for a few weeks. I planned to call you soon. So, what have you been up to?"

"Oh, the usual stuff, but I have some news. I have a singing gig at a nightclub in a couple of weeks, and was hoping you could come to support me. I suppose I'm asking too much since you're convalescing."

"It's in a fortnight? I might just surprise you and be able to go, so I won't say no, yet."

"Tell you what, over the weekend, Ill pop down to see you. Are you allowed company?"

"Yes. Come down. The country air will do you some good. You could bring some of your mother's famous Escovitch Chicken wings or even her Red Stripe chicken recipe, but damn, forget it. I can only eat soup and Jelly. Oh, I hate that stuff."

"That's a shame, but I can bring something for your parents. My mother loves to cook. I'll look up the train schedule from Victoria Station, and I'll come and cheer you up."

"I'd like that."

"Good, shall see you soon." Giving the phone to her father, Carrie grinned.

"It's my tennis friend, Shania. She's coming down over the weekend. You'll like her. Shania sings. I'll have her entertain us. That's if she doesn't get nervous. She says that she can sing better in front of large crowds, so we'll just have to convince her to sing to us. Her family is from Jamaica, and her mother creates fantastic Jamaican foods. You'll see."

"Oh, that'll be great, trying food from another culture."

"Do you think she can stay the weekend?" asked Carrie. "I forgot to ask her to. Would you mind, Mum?"

"I think that would be very nice. I like meeting your friends."

"Okay, I'll get back to her."

"How about a bowl of old fashioned chicken soup? I made it last night just for you. I took out the chicken bones. It's plain. I have the hospital menu which states what we have to stick to. Okay, dear?"

"It's awful. I'll have to cross out the days on the calendar when I can eat real food. I'll be eating this stuff through September I suppose."

"Yes, you will. I'll heat up a bowl of soup minus the noodles."

Carrie began to feel sleepy, so she left the kitchen and snuggled up on the living room sofa. Oscar followed, climbing up beside her.

"Don't fall asleep. Your mother wants you to have the soup," said Gary, following her into the living room. But it was to no avail. Carrie closed her eyes.

Rita was about to fill a soup bowl when Gary snuck back to the kitchen. "Never mind dear, she's sleeping. Besides, it's time for dinner, and I'm hungry."

"Oh, all right. When do you think we should tell her about the inheritance? She'll be thrilled when she hears this news. She has the jewelry from my grandmother, and now your mother leaving her all that money, and something for our Larry in Australia. It's such a wonderful gift for both of them," said Rita.

"To think in just a few weeks it's our daughter's birthday. I told Mum to go visit the places she had read about in the travel section of the newspaper, but she refused. I can still see her pointing to Egypt, Israel, France, Spain, Africa, and several other countries on maps, and sites she wanted to visit, but refused to go. Maybe it was because she was a widow and had no one to travel with. Constantly, she talked about those rotten years her family went through. The Great Depression in the States was bad and it affected us in England. Her father was on the dole. So when my mother got a job she saved every penny. She kept all her knick-knacks and my old toys. I found them it the attic after she died. It's a shame she didn't travel. The Trust states that Carrie is to receive her inheritance on her twenty-first Birthday."

"Our daughter has much to learn. I've tried. You know how we've battled. What can we do? She thinks that money is the world. I'm worried."

"Maybe when she reaches twenty-one, she'll grow up a bit," said Gary, smiling. "We can't worry about it, can we? I've hired a financial advisor to be here when she receives the inheritance. My mother was determined that she not touch a penny for two months. Apparently, my mother wanted her to learn how to manage her new income. So the advisor will show her how to manage. That's that! Now, what about that chicken soup? It smells divine. Leave in the noodles."

"Okay, one bowl of chicken soup coming up," said Rita. "It looks like we'll be making a big party. Twenty-one is a big day in anyone's life, and by the looks of things, Carrie won't return to London until she's fully recovered, so we better get a list of who she wants to invite."

"Sounds like a good idea," said Gary, dipping a cracker into his soup.

Eleven

Mark's Ordeal

Mark Rosen strolled around the new addition at the Skylight Inn. The fountain with the statue of Eros gleamed, and guests sat around the fountain watching the water ripple and splash. He stepped along the path of exotic flowers and listened to the tourists' comments. Usually, his keen blue eyes were alert with anticipation, but today they had no luster. This last month he had spent time in therapy. Feeling a little better, he decided to venture out and play some golf.

Mark's doctor had suggested a counselor. There were the nights Mark could not sleep. There were the days he tried to work on the accounts, but numbers blurred in front of him, which caused him to quit and leave his work. He'd gone through all the questions on why and what he could have done to save his marriage, but Matilda refused to reconcile.

He blamed his mother who had chastised him for marrying Matilda. Mark had tried to prevent his mother from meddling, and he thought the problems between his wife and his mother were minor, but he knew it was only half the truth. Matilda had left him for someone else, and that someone was his brother-in-law, Richard Evergreen. He couldn't admit this to anyone. The embarrassment caused him to avoid questions his family asked. Eventually, he knew the day would arrive when he would tell them the truth. Meanwhile, he had fought with his mother and told her in flashes of anger she was to blame for the end of his marriage.

Mark parked his red convertible near the golf course. He stepped out of the car and pulled out his golf bag. Staring at the white clouds, he felt the warm sun and the soft breeze on his collar. Stretching, he lifted his golf clubs on his shoulder, ready to spend a day away from the hotel. His mind cluttered with Matilda's haunting words, and a feeling of hopelessness spread through him, but today he had made up his mind to block out the impending divorce.

Before meeting Matilda, he'd told others, he was a confirmed bachelor, and definitely not interested in the institution of marriage. But seeing Matilda for the first time, he'd found a love he thought would last until he died. At thirty-four, he had felt like a teenager, head over heels in love with a girl who was just twenty-one. Mark picked up his golf bag and looked up to see his caddy coming down the grassy hillside.

"Morning Mark, let me take that. I'm on time, I hope. Looks like a perfect Miami day, a good day to golf," said Robert, taking the golf clubs from Mark. He placed them in a golf cart.

"How are the plans going? Do you still want to become a marine and serve our country?" asked Mark, strolling onto the golf course.

"I hope to. Are you ready? The others are waiting."

"Okay," said Mark. "I'm not much of a player, but it looks like a good day to improve. Let's meet the gang."

The golfers greeted Mark. He shook their hands and along with their caddies, began the game.

* * * * *

Ron Rosen tied his shoe laces, ready for his morning walk along Miami Beach. He poked his hand in his jacket pocket to make sure his favorite cigar was there. Happy he hadn't forgotten it, he grinned. He had promised Hilda, his secretary of twenty-five years that he would not smoke in the office, and closed his ears to his family constantly telling him not to smoke. They had called him a hypocrite because throughout the Skylight Inn the no smoking sign ruled.

Summer months had been the off season, so the Rosen family spent their days watching the gradual materialization of the new addition. The family had discussed that the restaurant would be dedicated to the memory of Sarah, a light in her father's eye. Sarah had caused friction among her three brothers while growing up. It seemed to them their father spent more time with Sarah and not much with them, but in adulthood, the tension healed, and now Mark, Jay, and Aaron grieved for their sister.

With Sarah's death, Ron felt as though a bullet had crushed his heart. Unable to eat or run the Skylight Inn, his family had placed him under a doctor's care. He had lost weight and lay in bed for days. Mark took over the hotel and his brothers worked alongside him.

It was his grandchildren who had helped Ron pull through his depression. Richard flew in Jennie and Joey from Twinsburg, Ohio to Miami Beach on occasional weekends, and phoned their grandfather often. With Mark's wedding and the loveliness of his new daughter-in-law, Matilda, Ron had begun to smile. He liked to make others laugh, and soon began telling jokes to the tourists, and rediscovered his morning walk.

Ron approached the beach. He recalled his depression and remembered how Mark and Janet had kept the Inn from closing. He believed the hotel could not survive without Mark. He asked himself if a non-family member could maintain the hotel. Even though Mark had said he'd leave, Ron didn't believe him. Lighting a cigar, he puffed smoke into the sea air. He hardly noticed the seagulls or the pelicans flying above. Usually, he stopped to admire the sandpipers digging their beaks into the sand, and checked the protected turtles coming up to nest on the beach, but this morning, he saw only Mark's mournful eyes.

What could he do to console his son? Mark had not said why

Matilda had asked for a divorce. Was it because she wanted to stay in London? Question after question hounded him.

Reaching his house next to the Skylight Inn, he picked up the morning newspaper. Entering the front door, he aimed for the kitchen. Janet had brewed a full pot of coffee and had left to host The Rose.

"Everything looks normal," said Ron, "but Mark has a hole in his heart and none of us know why Matilda is divorcing him. All right, son, I'll be here when you need me. Just get back to being Mark," said Ron, pouring himself a mug of coffee.

Finishing, he put the mug down and climbed the stairs to the master bedroom to change his clothes. It was another day at running his hotel, and he knew he had to be ready to meet the tourists with a smile.

Twelve

The Discussion

Brian Price had worked many hours focusing on the fashion presentation for Yamzing's. He constantly checked his notes, underlining sentences in red ink. The day would soon arrive when he would meet managers, celebrities, and buyers from boutiques and large department stores. He had walked around the warehouse picking up bits of lint, and had called in the cleaning staff. Finally satisfied, he positioned the podium for the announcer. Folding his arms, he sat in a seat staring and hoping he had done everything necessary to make Yamzing's new fashion line successful.

With much haranguing and several phone calls, he signed up the famous model Susan Gladstone. Brian was pleased. Her busy European schedule had been tight, but Brian reached the right connections, and got Miss Gladstone to sign the contract. She planned to arrive in London one day before the event.

Relaxing in his office, he double checked his notes. Arranging the papers on the desk, he jumped up and rummaged in his drawer. He thought he had written an important telephone number on a note and placed it in the right hand drawer of his desk. Fumbling, he pulled out paper clips, odd notes, and mail, but not the note with the phone number. "What did I do with it? I can't find it anywhere. I swear I put it in this desk." Picking up his mobile phone, he dialed Frank Evan's extension. No one answered.

Swiftly, Brian got up. He left his office and hurried to Frank's.

The sign on the door said "Welcome: Bring Your Ideas." Brian tapped on the door.

"Come on in," called Frank. He put down his pen and looked up. "Hey, Brian, how goes it? Your big event is in a couple of days. Is there something you need that I can be of service?"

"Thanks. I'm okay. It's set up to go. It should go well. I heard that Carrie Adler is recuperating in her parents' home in the country. Her having her appendix out the other day shocked me. I just need the phone number of her parents."

"I can help you with that. I just happened to place it in my daily notes. Here it is," said Frank. "She won't return to the company for six weeks. I take it you're good friends."

"Yes, we're lunch buddies; but of late, I haven't had lunch with her. This new position does not always fit for a regular lunch hour."

"Yeah, I know how that goes. Here, I'll write it on my business card."

"Much obliged," said Brian as he took the card. "Will you be able to catch the fashion show?"

"I plan on it. It's my job to know everything going on with Yamzing's. Oh, when you talk to Carrie, give her my best wishes."

"Sure," said Brian as he left Frank's office.

Frank stretched and stood up. He approached the picture window that overlooked the city traffic. He studied the men and women in their business suits walking briskly along the pavement, carrying their briefcases. Looking at them, he knew they represented the bankers, lawyers, and leaders in London. Observing them, he was aware of his position. He liked his job and enjoyed having the opportunity to be creative.

Often, he flew as a sales representative to other countries to check on the company's merchandise. Traveling was the only time he could immerse himself in a different culture and search out souvenirs.

Inviting friends to his flat, he liked to explain why he chose specific pieces of artwork, which he displayed in various rooms. Standing by the window, he thought of Carrie. There was something about her that piqued his curiosity. He saw her as a girl full of spunk, her eyes questioning and curious. He saw her as fresh and pretty. He saw her as someone he'd like to know better.

"What is it about her? She's only been here three months, but I wish she was back," he said. He returned to his desk and picked up some memos, looked them over, and picked up his phone.

"Hello, Mr. Evans. Is there something I can get you?" asked his secretary in the outside office.

"Yes, I can't get away for lunch. Could you bring me up a sandwich from the deli down the street? Anything will do."

"Sure. What beverage would you like?"

"Coffee with no cream or sugar would be fine."

"Right, I'll be back before you know it."

"Thanks, Ruby. Put it on my tab."

"I'll do that, Mr. Evans."

Frank found his tinted rimmed glasses under some papers. He had ordered a new pair of contacts and didn't like waiting for them. The glasses caused a red mark at the bridge of his nose, so he kept pulling them off. Now he was forced to wear them.

With a tap on the door, Ruby entered with his lunch.

"Here you go. I got you a hot pastrami sandwich and a dill pickle with a side salad. I know you like that. Watch the coffee, the cup is piping hot."

"Ruby, you're perfect, thank you," said Frank, sweeping his black hair from his forehead.

"Oh, you're welcome, Mr. Evans. Do you need anything else?"

"Yep, a magic wand to catch up would be nice."

"Why don't you take a walk around the corner and stretch your legs a little after you eat? I like walking around our famous city. There's always something going on. I often take my lunch and sit on the steps of St Paul's Cathedral. I never get tired of looking at our historical buildings. Walking is good for the heart. It'll clear your mind."

"Now, why didn't I think of that? I could do with some fresh air. Good idea."

"Go for it," said Ruby, closing the door.

Frank finished his lunch and dumped the paper plate and cup into the waste basket. "I'll work late tonight. A walk sounds good." Frank put on his light gray raincoat and left his office.

At the Adler house the phone rang again. Gary answered. "The Adler Residence, hello, this is Gary."

"I'm Brian, a friend, who works with Carrie. How is she?"

"Hello, Brian. I'll let her tell you, herself."

"Here, Carrie, it's for you. I can't believe you have so many friends checking on you."

"Thanks, Dad."

"Hello, Carrie."

"It's you, Brian. What's up? Working hard? I bet you can't wait for the soccer season and get away from it for a while. Well, we didn't make lunch. Did we? My plan went upside down."

"It did. Sorry, you've had a bit of an ordeal, but as soon as you're up to it, we'll go out."

"I'm getting better. I have to rest for a few weeks, but I'll be celebrating my twenty-first Birthday party on October thirty-first. I'll be having a party down here. Would you like to come? It'll be a costume party. You can come as Charlie Chaplin, the old time silent film star. You know how you are always talking about those old silent pictures. You clown around just like him." She began laughing, but stopped due to some pain.

"Say, I like that laugh and I do miss it. I'd like to say yes, but with this new promotion, Yamzing's will be sure to have me plan something on that day. Could you change the date?"

"That's a thought, but I doubt it. Just make the effort. It'll be six weeks before I get back to work. It will be around the end of September. Do you suppose you can come and visit over a weekend?"

"Yeah, that's why I called. This Saturday is the fashion show, and I know how much you wanted to attend. I'll visit soon."

"That's fine. Shania's coming down. She'd make a great model for the show. Darn, I'd love to see the new fall collection. Oh, I hate missing out. I know if I attended, I'd be buying something that no one will dare wear in public except me and the very rich."

"It'll be on a video. I'll bring it, and you can view the show and select something."

"Oh, that's lovely."

"Okay, gotta go. I still have some last minute things to take care of. Get better."

"Sure. Thanks for calling, Brian."

Carrie put the phone back. "It's nice out there. I think I'll take a walk," she called out to her father.

"Walk? Well, you can a little, but not down that country lane. Here, I brought back some library books. Read something or knit. Your mother likes to do that. She's making me some warm gloves for winter. Give yourself time to get your strength back, and then I'll walk with you."

"I can't knit Dad, and never will. I'll do the crossword puzzle from the newspaper."

Thirteen

Vacation Day

Anne Smith took one last look around the flat and lifted her China Doll plant. She felt encouraged to see it bloom. She had tried to nourish her plants, but had been unsuccessful. The leaves on her plants often turned brown, curled up, and died. With this new one, she placed it by a big window. The result was her plant thrived. She lifted her treasure and took it to her neighbor. Relieved she had someone to care for her plant she rushed back to the flat.

Next on the list was delivering Nifty to her son's. She never thought of Eric as a guardian of her cat. Her concern was Eric having time to care for him. Working as an electrician and traveling throughout London, repairing loose wires, televisions, and computers kept him busy. He also had begun dating Betty, who Anne had not met and wanted to. Eric had phoned offering to care for Nifty while she and Josh traveled to Hawaii. She gratefully accepted. She rushed about the flat fluffing pillows, dusting, and vacuuming.

She picked Nifty up, attempting to put him in a carrier, but he took off. Dashing under the table and running around the coffee table, he stopped and crouched behind the couch. She tried to coax him with a toy. He refused to move. Lying on the floor with her arm outstretched, Anne tried to reach him. Not having any luck, she called out to Josh.

"What's the matter?" he asked, coming out of the bedroom, seeing Anne lying on the floor calling the cat. "Here, Nifty," she called, but her cat refused to move.

"He won't get in that thing, and I can't reach him," she yelled.

"I can see that," said Josh, pulling the sofa from the wall. Quickly, he nabbed Nifty.

Struggling together, they backed him into the carrier. Anne gave a big sigh and rushed to the kitchen cupboard and came back with a treat, but Nifty refused it.

"Oh, my God, just look at him. Oh, my poor cat," said Anne, falling on the armchair. Sitting there, she held her stomach. She tried not to laugh, but a roaring cackling caused tears to gush down her cheeks.

"What's going on with you?" asked Josh.

"Oh, my, I can't stop myself," she said, inhaling breaths. "What a sight we must have looked trying to get him in that. I was thinking if anyone saw us on camera, they would be hysterical. I thought we'd never do it. Whew, that was bloody hard. Well, we did. Thank God for that," said Anne calming herself. "Right, well, that's done. I better get myself together," she said, brushing cat hair off her clothes.

"Are you packed?" asked Josh, returning to the bedroom to finish his packing. Anne shook her head.

"I thought you finished. I'll take Nifty over to Eric's. It'll give you time to finish up. Make sure you have everything you need. Check the list."

"Fine, don't forget his cat food. Darn, I have him so spoiled. I have to phone Emily. She isn't too keen on me leaving the country. She thinks I should stay here like a statue and never go anywhere. She's always been that way. She wants me around all the time."

"I know that. Okay, with the traffic the way it is, driving to the East End will be a bit of a hassle," said Josh, picking up the carrier. I don't know exactly what time I'll be back. He looks plenty angry," said Josh watching Nifty swish his tail. "I'll be off then."

"Bye my darling cat, I'll miss you so much," said Anne.

She sat down and then got up to look over the passports. "Awful picture of me," she uttered, putting the passport down. Picking up the brochures, she viewed the sites that Josh had circled.

"Let me see, we're staying in a five star hotel, and Josh has arranged for a tour guide. We're flying to Honolulu, and he's marked Waikiki and Maui to tour. Maui has lots of bridges and waterfalls. He seems to want to explore the volcano at the National Park, locate the green sea turtles, and visit some historical sites. Well, all I can say is I better carry some moisturizer for my feet. It all looks amazing and so gorgeous. I don't suppose we'll cover everything, but I'll be happy if we stay at a resort and stare at the ocean and think of nothing. That's for me. I don't blame Josh for wanting to see as much as he can. He hasn't had a vacation in years. With his wife dying from that rotten breast cancer, had to have been a long nightmare for him."

Anne put the brochures aside. She closed her eyes imagining the wonders of Hawaii. "I better get back to packing. I'll get it all done before Josh returns." The phone rang, and the palms of her hands began to perspire. It stopped and then rang again. This time, she answered and bravely announced, "Anne Smith speaking."

"Mum, where were you?"

"Oh, it's you, Emily. I was just about to pack."

"Are you all right, Mum?"

"Of course I am."

"I was waiting for your phone call."

"Emily, I was going to ring you. Josh just took Nifty over to Eric's. Tomorrow is the big day. I can't imagine flying all those hours. I suppose people do it all the time. It's almost fifteen hours. I've never had time to read much, so I'll load up at the airport with a bunch of paper back books. I like mysteries, like Agatha Christie, and some of the romance books. That should keep me occupied."

"Mum, you should get your books on a Kindle. Then you wouldn't need to buy all those paperback books."

"Now don't get me started on all that stuff. I'm not interested, and never will be. I have to hold a book in my hands."

"Mum, you might just like reading in a different way."

"I'll think about it. Anyway, we'll be up with the birds tomorrow. We made up our minds to fly British Airways to Honolulu. I'm lucky I won the best waitress prize. It covers all expenses."

"Mum, it's all great. Have a wonderful time. I'm still upset over Nifty, but I know Eric will take good care of him. I'm sorry about the accident he had while he was with me."

"Emily, stop worrying about that. I've even got used to his half tail. I'll bring you back a nice present, something made in Hawaii."

"Mum, don't. Just enjoy yourself. You work hard at Charlene's restaurant."

"I'll see if there's something I like. I better pack. Josh will be back before I know it. I'm putting in the address book first. I'll do what Matilda does. I'll send a postcard to all of you."

"That'll be nice, Mum."

"All right love. I'll say bye. See you in a fortnight."

Fourteen

Goldie's Predicament

Mark Rosen sat in the Rose restaurant wearing his sunglasses. Taking them off, he looked around. He had been proud of his decorating, and often heard positive remarks about the décor which pleased him. But today, his eyes looked empty, and his facial expression drawn. Around the fountain, women threw in nickels, dimes, and quarters, then made a wish. Mark watched the money sink to the bottom. People who came to the Skylight Inn were aware the donations were going to charity. Mark gathered up the coins each month and mailed a check to the armed forces for the wounded American veterans and soldiers.

Tourists sat at the tables eating, smiling, and talking to each other. Nonchalantly, Mark sipped his coffee that Mary, the head waitress, had brought over. His blank stare replaced his usual mischievous grin, and his face remained void of humor. Unsmiling, he looked up to see the new waitress approaching with a coffee pot. Goldie hesitated, not wanting to disturb Mark. Mary had told her to ask if he would like a menu. Goldie picked up one and headed for Mark's table.

"Hello, Mr. Rosen," said Goldie. "Ready for lunch?" Her dimples and beaming smile and her upbeat voice warmed up the patrons. Mark glanced at her and grinned.

"How you doing with the coffee?" she asked.

"Hi, Goldie. I don't need a refill yet."

"All right then. I'll leave the menu. It's going to be a nice day," she said. "I'll be back in a few minutes to check on you."

"Fine," said Mark.

Waitresses had been gossiping all morning, knowing that Mark had been at court to discuss his divorce. Mary had told them to mind their business and concentrate on serving the tourists and not embarrass Mark when he came in. Mary was indispensable. She could run the Rose on her own, and she had recently trained Goldie. She hoped Goldie would stay. At first, Goldie had hesitated on approaching Mark.

Goldie had a college degree in liberal arts, and hadn't made up her mind what her future career might be. She had studied languages and was fluent in Spanish and French. Having resided in the Cleveland area in Ohio and graduated from Kent State, she was now enjoying the sunshine, and swimming on her days off. She wanted to take a break from seriously looking for a job for about a year, and she couldn't think of a more exciting place than Miami Beach, so she took a job as a server. She disliked the snow and ice in the winter months in Ohio, and no matter how many sweaters she wore when going out, she never felt warm.

At the Skylight Inn, she felt welcome, and tourists liked chatting to her. She shared her experiences with the guests and gave them good service. Consequently, the Rosen's were pleased she worked for them.

Goldie's family often moved due to her father serving in the armed forces. He had just returned from Afghanistan and was now based in North Carolina. In her growing years, Goldie's four older brothers had spent time protecting her.

She wanted to be freer, so she had decided Florida would suit her. But there were days she didn't get the big tips, so she skipped dinner every other night, and breakfast was a slice of toast, and occasionally a bowl of cereal. Her money was short. She found herself continually opening a chest drawer and counting, making decisions on what she could or could not spend. She thought she might call her father and explain her predicament, but knew his answer would be to return home; so she didn't make the phone call.

Goldie approached Mark again. "Hi, ready for the delicious lentil soup? The rumor is Aaron has become quite the chef, and I haven't had the opportunity to meet him. I have to tell him what our customers are saying. Everyone likes his soup. Would you like a bowl or a cup?"

Mark put down his coffee mug and stared. "Okay, Goldie, I'll have to introduce him to you. You know what? I'm really hungry. I can't remember when I last ate. A bowl would be fine."

Mary glanced over at Goldie and saw she was smiling. "Looks like Goldie is going to be good for Mark today," she said, wiping up a table. "Lord knows what that man has been through."

Goldie returned with the soup. "Here you go. Enjoy," she said.

"Thank you, Goldie. We appreciate having you here. The customers like you."

"Oh, thank you, Mr. Rosen," said Goldie, returning to see Mary waving at her to come over.

"How is he?" Mary asked.

"He seems fine and is eating."

"How do you like working for us? Do you think you'll be around a while?" asked Mary.

"Well, I don't know for sure. Do you have a minute to talk?"

"Sure, lunch hour will be over in about an hour. I'll meet you in the back room."

"Okay, I'll check on Mark to see if he wants anything else."

"Good," said Mary.

Goldie returned to Mark's table and saw that he was fine.

Mark finished his lunch and strolled around the restaurant and then left.

The restaurant crowd began to dissipate and waitresses wiped down the tables while the busboys swept up the floor.

Goldie went to the back room where Mary was checking up on the silverware. "Okay, we've got through the lunch hour, so what did you want to ask me?"

"Oh, I had something on my mind, but it isn't important."

"Are you sure?"

"Yes, it can wait."

"Okay then. You can clock out. I know you're dying for some of that sunshine, right?"

"I am. Bye, see you tomorrow."

Mary smiled. She continued to think about Mark. Finding a soft cloth and polish, she cleaned the silver. She disliked seeing him at the table with his shoulders hunched over and his eyes looking down.

"It's all a puzzle to me what went wrong with those two. I suppose none of us will ever know," she said, finishing up polishing a spoon. "I wish I could do something for Mark."

The next day, Goldie met with Mary and told her the predicament she was in. After their conversation, Mary told Goldie to speak to Mr. Rosen for more working hours. Ron Rosen was glad to help. After much discussion, Ron decided that Goldie could work at the front desk in the evenings and help those who visited from countries who spoke French or Spanish. He saw her as an asset.

Fifteen

A Heartache

Matilda read the statement that said her divorce should be finalized in December. She shifted her chair and got up to stretch and think. Her mind became empty, and she could not concentrate. "This is all too much. It's endless, I'm so tired."

In her small rented furnished apartment by Kent State in Ohio, she was finishing up her last course of study before she was to do her student teaching. She had transferred her courses to Kent State from Miami Florida after her move to the Cleveland area. Staring at the phone, she called Richard. Tears welling, and her body shaking, she heard Richard say hello. She blurted out his name. Unable to form another word, she dropped the phone.

Trying to call Matilda, Richard kept hearing a busy signal As it was a Saturday afternoon, and his children were playing with friends at his neighbors, he asked them to watch his children for a little while. He returned to his house grabbed his car keys and drove to Matilda's apartment.

With the death of Sarah, Richard spent his days in a fog. Matilda, who came from London, graduated from a nanny school in Ohio and was hired by Richard's mother to care for his children. She organized his home. Joey and Jennie became attached to her. Matilda read to them, painted with them, listened to them, laughed with them, and comforted them. The children depended on her, but Richard had not anticipated Matilda would marry Mark Rosen after knowing him a short time. Nor had he accepted that he was in love with her, and that she would move to Miami Beach, Florida where Mark helped run the Skylight Inn

And so it was on an annual visit to his in-laws at the Skylight Inn while driving to a drug store, that Richard had a head-on car collision, leaving him in a coma. He spent weeks recovering in a Florida hospital. Matilda took Joey and Jennie to visit their father and sat by Richard's bedside waiting for a sign of movement.

One afternoon, awakening from his coma, Richard saw Matilda. Semi-conscious, he glanced over and confessed his love for her. When she heard his comments, she assumed he did not mean what he was saying, but sitting for days, watching the clock tick, the hours crawl, and praying for him, she knew she had bonded with Richard.

By the following summer, Richard recovered and was back in Twinsburg running his business. Because Matilda had been a nanny to his children, Matilda's mother invited Richard to her wedding to Josh Smith in London. Matilda attended without Mark. He could not leave due to his heavy schedule at the Skylight Inn.

Meeting Richard again, Matilda became shaky. She did not have the courage to face her feelings, but knew she had to. She reminded Richard that he had said he loved her. He had laughed at her remarks and casually said he was fond of her because of the kindness and the care she had given his children. Matilda was mystified by his denial of his love for her and asked him to admit his true feelings, but he left London without a word. He returned to Twinsburg, but Matilda remained unconvinced and decided to end her marriage to Mark.

In the past, Richard had been chivalrous, not wanting to break up her marriage. On a long distance phone call, Matilda told him she loved him. With thousands of miles between them, he crumbled and finally admitted he loved her. Immediately, he flew back to London to escort her to Twinsburg.

Remembering all that had occurred in just a few months, Matilda felt guilty about how she had treated Mark. She had not wanted to hurt him, but she no longer loved him, so could not remain in her marriage.

Tears soaked the new pillow slip. Catching her breath, she tried to stop crying, but her sobs continued. Finding some strength, she climbed out of the bed and entered the bathroom to bathe her swollen eyes. Returning to the kitchen, she put the receiver back. She tried to clear her thoughts, but the ringing of the doorbell forced her to venture down the stairs. Peeking through a keyhole in the front door, she saw Richard. Relieved, she opened the door. He stood there smiling, pulled her close and held her in his arms.

"My darling Matilda, what's wrong? The connection went dead. I lost you. It will be all right. I'm here. You'll be free soon. Are you all right?"

"Yes," she said. He held her close. Resting her head on his shoulder, she closed her swollen eyes. She then looked up at him. "I love you so much," she said, breaking into a smile.

Sixteen

Certain Memories

The Smiths had been back in London from their Hawaii trip one week when Anne saw the postman approach her mail box. She rushed out and greeted him, and the postman placed the letters in her hands.

"Thank you, nice morning. Enjoy this bit of sunshine. We were gone a fortnight, and I have to tell you Hawaii was smashing, and there was not a sign of the constant rain we have. I highly recommend going there if you ever get a chance."

The postman smiled. "I don't think that's possible for now, but it was a bit of all right then?"

"It was. We had a jammy time."

"Good, welcome back home."

"Thank you, we're happy to be back."

"How's that great cat of yours?" he asked.

"Not too good right now. He's moping lots."

"I suppose cats get upset too when you leave them."

"They do indeed," said Anne. "When Nifty came back from Eric's, he hid behind the drapes. Our son said Nifty was fine with him, and there were no problems."

"He'll adjust again," laughed the postman walking on to the next house.

Sorting through the mail in the kitchen a postcard fell. Anne snapped it up and saw Matilda's writing and a picture of downtown Cleveland. Feeling her heart pound, she sat in her armchair and read.

"Dear Mom, Just want to tell you the divorce will be over in a few months. I'm doing fine, and I'll write a long letter soon. Love, Matilda."

"Well, I suppose it's taking longer than she thought. Now what? I hope she doesn't get married again in another rush."

Propping the card on her kitchen counter, Anne checked the time and decided to phone Carrie. Due back at the Charlene restaurant on Monday, Anne felt she needed time to sort through all the photos she planned for an album. The waitresses would want to see them, and her boss Mike expected an account of the trip. He had initiated the waiter's contest and Anne was grateful she had won.

Carrie answered the phone. "Anne, I'm glad you're back. How was Hawaii?"

Anne gleefully talked of her travels like a school child on a first outing. Once she began telling her adventures, she could not stop.

"I'm glad you had a good time," said Carrie. "I'll be back in my job in three weeks. It'll be something for me to handle. I'm still a little tired. Do you have any news from Matilda?"

"Yes, I do. I just got a postcard. Her divorce will be over soon, it seems."

"Oh, I see. Is she going to get married as soon it's over?"

"I don't know. Richard is a good man, but I'm hoping she'll finish up her degree first. She said she'll be writing more information in a letter. Okay, Carrie, we'll see you in London soon, and we'll do our marketing on a Saturday as usual. Get stronger each day."

"I hope to," said Carrie, putting the phone down. She looked at her mother.

"What's going on?" said Rita.

"It's Anne, they're back from Hawaii."

"How'd she like it?"

"She said she loved it, but the big news is that Matilda sent her a postcard and said her marriage will be over soon."

"Oh my, I don't know whether to laugh or cry."

"Mum, do neither."

"Here, a parcel just arrived. It's addressed to you."

"How come it came here?" Carrie rolled her eyes and saw the handwriting. "I'd know that writing anywhere. It's from Matilda. Anne must have told her that I'm recovering with my family."

"She did," said Rita, grinning.

Rapidly, Carrie opened the small package. In it, she found a silver charm bracelet with a pretty gift card wishing her good heath, and telling her how much she was missed.

"Oh, how lovely," said Carrie as she fingered the bracelet. A Rembrandt charm of a terrier that resembled her dog, adorned the bracelet.

"I love it," she said, as she jangled the bracelet on her right wrist. "It fits so nicely. How thoughtful. I miss her, too."

"I know you do," said her mother, smiling. "It would be nice if you could visit her. She needs you."

"With all the things I'm planning, it'll take me years to get there."

"Who knows? Maybe it won't." It was then Rita gasped, for she had almost told Carrie about the inheritance, but stopped herself from ruining the secret.

Carrie became quiet. She sat there thinking. Her thoughts were on her friend. She knew that nothing would ever interfere with her friendship with Matilda, even though she had been upset with Matilda's lifestyle. Although Matilda was thousands of miles away, Carrie knew she must be there for her. Looking over the bracelet, Carrie remembered when they were teens in school exchanging clothes, writing notes in class, and she herself cheating on tests. It was Matilda who had told her she was wrong to do that. Carrie had listened to Matilda and learned to respect her. It was a friendship that continued to blossom. Many memories remained, and Carrie thought of some of the antics they had got into. "Mum, as soon as I'm up to it, I'll add some charms. Matilda couldn't have sent a nicer gift. Do you think we could phone her tomorrow?"

"Do you have her phone number?"

"No. I'll call Anne in the morning."

"Sounds like a good idea. How about a slow walk around the lane with Oscar? I think you're ready."

"Mum, I am. I'm crossing off the days on that dog calendar you gave me. I can't wait to return to London, I suppose it will be back to Yamzing's. I need the money."

"I know. In a couple of weeks you can eat solid food. So what foods have you really missed the most?"

"That's easy. It's your homemade biscuits I've seen dad gobble up. Where's dad?" Carrie asked.

"He's down at the pub playing darts and having a beer, and I bet he's discussing world events and what's wrong with our government. He never tires of that subject. Are you ready to stroll?"

"Mum, I'm more than ready."

"Oscar, come here. We're going for a walk. Darn, it's raining again. Do you still want to go?"

"Of course, I love the rain, but Oscar hates it. He won't put one paw out."

"I know; he's going to hide," said Rita, putting on her raincoat.

Seventeen

The Singer

An announcer introduced Shania and told the audience this was her debut at the Palm Jazz club and would be singing some old standards. He asked the audience to give Shania a hand. Staring at the audience and feeling apprehensive, Shania adjusted the microphone. In a rented gown of red silk with a long slit in the front, wearing her mother's pearl necklace, and new black high heels, Shania trembled. Glancing toward the front tables, she saw her mother, Carrie, and a friend from work, Brian Price. A trumpet blew and the small group of musicians who had practiced with Shania brought out the sounds of the guitar, piano, tenor sax, and bass. A spotlight shone. She hesitated, then began singing a classic Louis Armstrong number, "Body and Soul." She then sang 'Sophisticated Lady" by Duke Ellington and finished with "Embraceable You" by George and Ira Gershwin. At the end of the performance, the audience gave her a warm applause. Feeling an instant glow, and a lot calmer, Shania left the stage.

"That was just amazing," said Carrie, looking across the table at Shania's mother.

"She liked the songs I played on the old stereo. When she was a kid, she would sing along with Ella Fitzgerald, Rosemary Clooney, Judy Garland, and so many others. I collected lots of records. She did good, didn't she?" said Mrs. Della.

"I'd say," said Carrie, looking up at the waiter who brought her dinner. "Hey everyone, I'm actually going to eat a real meal. Thank you," she said to the waiter who was elegantly attired in a black suit, bow tie, and white shirt.

"That's good. How are you feeling?" said Mrs. Della.

"I'm doing fine and will return to work next week."

"And you'll be playing tennis again, too. Oh, here comes Shania. Come sit down. You did so good, baby," said Mrs. Della.

"Oh, Mum, you think so?"

"Think so? I know so. I bet you're hungry. You ate hardly a bite today."

"I'm wondering if the manager will have me back. He said he'd tell me after the performance." Shania glanced about the club. "Where is he?"

"Oh, he's probably occupied with something," said her mother. "Here's the menu. Pick something."

"Not yet. I have to wait for the manager."

"Shania, you ate nothing today."

"Oh, mum, I just have to know what he thinks."

"Patience, patience," said her mother, looking around. An elderly gentleman approached. He was dressed in a navy striped suit, pink shirt, and a plaid tie. A boutonniere of a red carnation was in his lapel.

"Hello, young lady. May I thank you for the songs you just sung? They brought back so many happy memories, and your voice is so moving. That was delightful."

Shania, looking surprised, said thank you.

"I'm a big jazz fan. I used to play in a band all hours of the night. I played the saxophone. Those were the days."

"I know what you mean," said Mrs. Della, and proceeded to tell the man about her old record collection.

"That's great," said the stranger. Well, Miss Shania, I'll be here to see you every night, and I'll bring my friends. I must be off. These days I do need to get my rest," he said. Holding his walking stick, he maneuvered to the exit door. All at the table watched him leave.

"See," said Carrie. "You have lots to offer. I'm sure everyone here felt the same way as that gentleman."

Shania giggled and picked up the menu. She beckoned the waiter to come over and ordered.

"Mum, I'm half starved."

"I knew it," said her mother.

The manager, Mr. Vincent, had been standing in the back of the club watching Shania and talking to a regular customer "Well, how'd you like that young girl?" he asked.

"I liked her just fine."

"I did too. I suppose I'll have her stay on the week."

"She's got something about her. I'll come back and see her."

"You will? That's good. I suppose I'd better tell her she's got the whole week."

"If I were you, I'd tell her she's got the whole month of September. That girl can sing, and she's not bad to look at."

"Thanks," said Mr. Vincent, patting the man's shoulder. Walking over to Shania, she turned to watch him coming toward her.

He smiled and waved to the customers as he approached Shania. She sat still, her eyes blazing at Mr. Vincent.

"Okay, Shania, you'll be here for the whole week. Make sure you get here on time. We can't keep our customers waiting."

"Oh, I'll be here," said Shania, seeking her mother's hand. Mr. Vincent left the table and hurried to the kitchen.

Carrie got up and hugged Shania. "We have to celebrate. Do you suppose we can share a dessert?"

"How about some champagne now?" asked Brian.

"No, Carrie, you can't touch that yet," said Mrs. Della.

"You're right, and that's one thing I'm not interested in. I don't drink alcohol. I can order a soda," said Carrie.

"Okay, sounds good," said Mrs. Della.

"I suppose I'll have to order that, too," said Brian smiling.

"Well, I'd like dessert later," said Shania.

"Okay," said Brian, looking for the waiter to come back to the table.

Eighteen

At Yamzing's

Carrie returned to her job. She had contemplated the idea of not coming back to Yamzing's, but with her finances draining, she knew she had to. Sitting at her desk, she stared at the paperwork. It was then she saw a female employee approaching. Carrie quivered.

"How are you? I work over there," said the young woman, pointing to where her desk was located. "I came to help when you collapsed. We were so worried. I called for an ambulance. Anyway, let me introduce myself. I'm Regina and am pleased to see you back. If there's anything you need today, just ask."

"I'm fine, and I appreciate all that you did," said Carrie, looking down at her paperwork.

"I've brought you a plain doughnut and some coffee. Can you eat it?"

"Oh, thanks, I can," said Carrie. Regina smiled at her, then left after placing the doughnut and coffee on the desk.

Carrie's stomach flip flopped. She knew this was the beginning of more questions to come. She thought to herself. "I should have said more to her. She helped save my life."

Holding the coffee cup, sipping a little, and finishing the doughnut, she hesitated to start working. But everyone was busy. Picking up a file, she pulled out a paper. Relieved that no one else popped over, she immersed herself in her job and did not stop working until twelve. It was then she pulled back her chair, tidied her desk and looked up. Coming toward her desk was the manager, Frank Evans.

With his black hair shining and wearing a smile, he stopped at her desk. "Hello, Carrie. How are you this morning? It's good to see you looking well. We've missed you and are glad you're back."

"Oh, I'm fine, Mr. Evans and happy to be back."

"Good to hear," said Frank. "Don't forget to go for lunch."

Practically choking and trying to find the right words to say, she did her best to avoid Frank's eyes. "Um, Mr. Evans, I just want to thank you for all you did for me."

"Don't think about it. We're pleased you're okay. You had us scared for a few minutes, but you look like you're fine, so that's what counts."

"Mr. Evans, I'm truly grateful."

"Just glad I was of some help. Take it easy today." He turned away and walked on to the next desk to speak to another employee.

"Oh, God, I'm glad that's over," she mumbled to herself. Picking up her lunch in a red paper bag, Carrie took the lift down to the cafeteria. Yawning, she found an empty table. Looking up, she saw Regina approaching.

"Carrie, I'd like to join you. I hope you don't mind. I must apologize. I should have welcomed you to Yamzing's a lot sooner. You were here for three months, and I missed the opportunity to introduce myself. I've been here two years, and love working for this company. Mr. Evans is a great boss. He takes time to explain what he wants. The last job I had was very bad. How are you feeling?"

"I'm a little tired. I'll just have to get used to the pace I suppose."

"Have you come back too soon?"

"No, the doctor released me, and said I could go back to work. Just settling back to a routine and getting organized is a task."

"I imagine it is. Tell me what you'd like to eat. I'll get it for you."

"I'm fine. I packed lunch."

"Would you like a cold drink? Tell me what you'd like."

"A soda any kind would be fine."

"Okay, I'll see what they have."

Carrie sat back. The table began to fill with Yamzing's employees. Suddenly, a chair pulled up beside her. She turned around and found herself staring at Frank Evans who sat down next to her.

"Hello, Carrie, I decided it was time for lunch. How was your morning?" he asked, his eyes as pleasing as a spring day.

"It's been fine. Regina is bringing me a drink."

"Good. How did the morning go?"

"It went well."

"I'm glad to hear that. I'll see what the cafeteria has to offer," said Frank, moving his chair back.

"I've got you some ginger ale. It's getting busy," said Regina, putting her tray on the table.

"Thank you, you're most kind," said Carrie.

"My pleasure."

"Mr. Evans is joining us," said Carrie.

"Oh, that's good. He's fun."

"Is he really fun?" asked Carrie.

"Yeah, just when you're having a hard day, he'll come over and tell a joke, and when he does this, I end up laughing. It takes the edge off when under pressure. Oh, here he comes."

"Hello, ladies, they have my favorite today, Shepherd's Pie."

"It looks tempting," said Regina.

Carrie watched Frank. While she couldn't bring herself to mingle in the conversation, a feeling of contentment swept though her. She ate her egg salad sandwich and smiled at him, aware of a kinship she'd never expected.

Nineteen

A Translator

Mark Rosen greeted Goldie at the front desk of the Skylight Inn. "Hi, how's the girl doing that speaks French and Spanish to our tourists?" he asked, checking the reservations on the computer. "We seem to have you working all over the place, and now you're here for the evening shift. We like you around here. My mother's said you make our customers happy."

"Thank you, Mark. "I'm looking forward to speaking to the tourists. I'll get stale in Spanish if I don't use the language. I was thinking of going back to a university in Ohio to work on a master's degree in public relations once I earn some money for classes."

"You do that, Goldie," said Mark, shuffling papers. "We have a busload of tourists from out of state coming in soon. Keep a watch for the bus. When it arrives, we'll probably have a long line, so we'll have you help settling them in. Has anyone shown you how our cash register works yet?"

Goldie fidgeted. She knew lots about computers, but had not worked a cash register.

"No. I'm sorry, Mark, I am not familiar with that yet."

"No? Oh, I wasn't thinking. This is the first time you've come to the Skylight Inn's front desk. Some guests might need you to translate. When you do, remember to tell them the best food is here at our hotel. They need to know ours is the tops. Okay?"

"I'll be sure to tell them that."

"Good. Okay, I'm off. I have things to do. Aaron is finishing up in the Rose kitchen. I'll just text him to get him here. If he can't make it, I'll get Jay to help out."

Goldie approached the counter. She knew she must learn the register and fast. After setting her purse behind the counter, she watched the tourists go in and out of the hotel. She loved working at the Skylight Inn and wished to stay longer. Now she hoped by working the extra hours, her income would stretch. She got on well with Janet, who had treated her like a daughter.

The old wind-up clock on the wall struck the hour. Goldie glanced across the lobby at the swinging glass doors. A young man entered.

"You must be Goldie."

"Yes, that's me."

"Excuse my appearance. I'm Aaron. I have to get to the men's room and clean up." Returning he looked better having brushed off the flour that had spilled down his shirt, hair, and jeans which Goldie had tried not to laugh at when first seeing him.

"Mark said to get over here fast. I've been making French dishes at the Rose. The French chef my mother hired last year has shared his recipes with me; and now I'm almost a decent cook. Our clients enjoy French cuisine. I've heard you speak the language fluently, but don't try it on me. I have no flare for languages, except for a few French words and phrases. Anyway, welcome. I've heard you've been with us a while."

"Oh, no, it's not too long. So, you are a cook? That's great. Cooking and I don't agree. I burn stuff. I've been studying Spanish since first grade. At my mother's insistence I added French in high school and at the university. I've heard that Florida is practically bilingual. I thought learning two languages would be useful in a career and especially here."

81

"That's great you did that. Okay, let's get ready for the onslaught. You can watch me at the register to get the swing of it."

"Okay, fine," said Goldie.

"According to my watch, the bus should roll in any minute. You can greet our guests at the door when they arrive."

Goldie stood next to Aaron at the register, but just as he was to give her the first lesson a grinding screech was heard. "Oops, we better make it another time. Here's the bus."

Goldie rushed to the door. The passengers entered and Goldie heard a language she didn't connect with.

"Aaron," she called, "I'm lost. I can't get what they are saying. I'm guessing it's Russian."

"Okay, we'll muddle through, but there'll probably be some tourists that'll be glad you can translate for them. I'll have you direct people to their rooms. We have no bellhop. Dennis is off for the day, so I guess you're it."

"Fine," said Goldie. "I'll do my best, but my sense of direction is not good."

"No problem, here's a map. If all else fails, wing it."

Goldie laughed. She certainly was working all over at the Skylight Inn, but was glad she did not have to call her father. She knew she had to make the two jobs work.

A middle-aged couple approached. The woman began speaking. She threw her hands in the air and her voice got louder. Goldie recognized the visitor was speaking in French. Calmly, Goldie responded in French. The gentlemen kissed her hand. Goldie was amazed and relieved her French skills had worked. She guided a couple to the desk. Aaron ran the register and checked them in while Goldie greeted other tourists, and had them go to the desk to check in. She looked over at Aaron.

"I'm not sure where to take the guests to their rooms, Aaron, I'm sort of lost. I don't think I can do well at this. I don't want to confuse the guests."

"Just hang in. You'll make it," said Aaron, grinning. "There are just a few hallways. Remember, the doors have numbers."

"I know that part," called Goldie, struggling down the hallway to help carry the tourists' suitcases.

Twenty

Hilda's Demands

Ron Rosen left his office after leaving a note for his secretary, Mrs. Hilda Davidson, who was out on an errand. He considered her his collaborator, his consoler, his decision maker, and simply the best secretary, having worked for him for twenty-five years. Hilda had complained her vacation had been delayed for too long, and she demanded a break now or she would leave. With that statement, Ron knew he had better find temporary help as fast as possible. This was on his mind as he strolled over to admire the finishing touches on the new edition.

The sun lit up the lobby, and through the glass door, the crystal chandelier sparkled. Standing outside, Ron stood by the palm trees and the new flower beds designed by a hired landscaper who took pride in creating specific areas to make the flowers eye catching. Content, Ron turned and walked in the direction of his house.

On his walk, he stopped to talk to tourists who commented to him about the beauty and comfort of the Skylight Inn, and it was then Sarah crept into his thoughts. He would miss her forever. Even now he could see her face, her sharp blue eyes, her red hair, and her enthusiasm for everything she did. Her portrait and the paintings she created, hanging in the lobby, gave him some relief from his sadness. His beloved daughter, a young mother who had lived her life with joy, was gone. She had been swallowed away from him, but now he was beginning to adjust.

In the distance, he observed his son Jay examining the landscape, and it seemed to Ron that Jay showed more interest in the family business, which had been the total opposite position when he had left the Skylight Inn. Ron prayed Jay's gambling days were over. Jay disappearing without a word had the family in chaos searching for him. With his return, Ron had decided to stay by him and get him help to recover from his addiction.

Having Jay back and seeing him checking the soil and grass, and conversing with the family about family matters had Ron walking about the grounds with a slight grin on his face. He had heard Jay was beginning to pay up his gambling debt. Reaching the house, he cleared his mind, ready to tell Janet about Hilda's ultimatum.

Entering the kitchen, he saw Janet making a turkey sandwich. Ron poured some coffee into his favorite mug.

"Well, it's nice it's all over."

"What's all over?" said Janet.

"The opening of our new addition and having that rock star Bill Jenkins entertain. We were lucky to have him. It was a great day."

"We were fortunate. You're earlier than usual. Is everything all right at the office?'

"It is. Ah, that sandwich looks good. I'm getting hungry."

"Open the refrigerator and you'll find one I made for you. I have to eat fast. Imagine, in this hot weather we have a waitress out with a virus. I suppose she has laryngitis, which is too bad. It must be that. Her voice sounds like a frog croaking. So I'd better get to The Rose on the quick."

"Okay, but can you spare a minute?"

Janet poured herself a glass of lemonade. "Yes, a quick minute," she answered, downing her drink and closing the refrigerator.

"Hilda is upset. She said she'll leave now if she doesn't get her vacation right away, and I can't have that."

"Oh, she's just kidding you! She won't leave us. But she is right. She deserves not only a vacation but something special on our part to celebrate the twenty-five years she's worked for us."

"Of course, why didn't I think of that?"

"I was thinking we should ask if she would like to travel somewhere."

"She never struck me as someone that enjoys traveling. She always tells me she would like to sit on her outside swing and do nothing for a while and spend some time with her grandchildren. She said she wants to take them to the zoo. I can't let her quit yet."

"Ron, she's just letting off steam. She won't leave. I'll drop over and tell her she can take her vacation next Monday. It's the last week in September, a good time for a break. It's Mark we have to think about. Has he said anything more about leaving us?"

"No."

"We just have to give him time to heal," said Janet with a guilty look.

"I suppose so. Okay, I'll guess I'll eat that sandwich; and I'll tell Hilda you'll be dropping over to discuss her vacation."

"Right, that's the plan," said Janet as she hurried out.

Ron sat back, eating a dill pickle. He thought about all the changes that had occurred in just a few short months. He liked Matilda from the moment he'd met her. He questioned why she was divorcing Mark. Would Mark ever share this with him? All he knew was that he wanted his brilliant son back to running the hotel with his business sense and creative ideas.

"I'll just wait it out a little longer to have a long talk," said Ron. "And then he'll tell me. I know."

He finished his black coffee and wiped his mouth with a paper napkin, put his dishes in the kitchen sink, then poured in some dish washing liquid. Janet had asked him not to leave dirty dishes on the table. Domesticated he was not. "Let them soak," she had said.

"I'll pick a day and clean it all out of him just like those dishes soaking. I'll get Mark to open up." Ron left with a look that said he had solved a dilemma. His anxious expression turned to a look of contentment as he closed the back door and strolled to his office.

"Hilda, what's up?" asked Ron poking his head into her office, glad that she was back from her errand.

"I'm finishing up the letter you asked me to send out to your Kiwanis club. You know; the notice to remind the club members that you'll be having the Continental Circus at Christmas for the second year to raise money for our wounded soldiers."

"Yes, that's good. The community will bring their families, and we'll raise plenty for our troops. We did great at the last event. Our soldiers need all the help we can give them. They're our heroes. Don't forget to announce the date in the paper. Let the media know we hire our vets at the Skylight Inn."

"I'll do that next."

"Hilda, Janet will be coming over soon to discuss your vacation. We don't want you leaving us."

Hilda grinned, "I'm not leaving. I just want you to get a jump on it."

"Good! I'm calling the temporary service today. I'll have someone over in a couple of days." In his pocket he fingered his cigar. He had heard Hilda and Janet complain so many times about his bad habit so decided to smoke elsewhere, and not the office. He knew it was against the law to smoke in any public building, so he stopped after being caught by Hilda who often reprimanded him.

"Okay, Hilda, you've got everything under control, so I'm off for a little while. I'll sign that letter when I get back."

She stared at him with a curious expression and returned to the computer.

Ron strolled toward the sea. He dug in his pocket and pulled out the cigar, lit it, took a deep breath and gazed at a boat with its white sail drifting. Ron stood there lost in the vastness of his surroundings. The ocean answered his question on why he had chosen to live in Miami Beach, Florida where he had built his dream, the Skylight Inn. He watched the giant waves beating against the shore. It was on days like this when the sky was not threatening with darkening clouds, indicating a storm might arise, that he felt calm and free.

Twenty-0ne

An Outing

Carrie and Anne had not met for a while for their usual Saturday market days where they would buy fresh fish, fruit, and barter with the vendors for the best price of the day. It was on these occasions they exchanged gossip, with Anne mostly sharing and discussing her opinions on the environment. Instead of marketing, the two sat on a park bench at London's famous Regent's Park. The sky was a pale, smoky blue and the oak trees surrounding the river bed offered cool shelter from the sun.

The thick green lawns captured the attention of all that strolled through the park. Scattered deckchairs held sleeping visitors, seeking the sun. Enamored with the idea of a simple day of relaxing and drinking in the pleasures of the park, the two chatted.

Carrie, having fully recovered from her surgery, was bursting to share her daily activities. Her eyes were alight as she gazed out at the swans gliding along the river. She commented on the tourists snapping photographs. Hearing the different languages, she tried to guess what country the travelers were from. She asked Anne if she might know.

Anne, looking surprised, said, "Don't ask me. I've no idea, not the slightest."

On days like this, Carrie felt that London was the greatest city in the world, even though she had heard that Paris and New York were exciting too.

"It's nice we have some sun today," she said to Anne who was taking off her sandals, stretching her feet, and twitching her toes.

"This is the place to be. The grass is so soft; I could walk barefoot. Even though I work down that side street, I don't get a chance to sit here. Hawaii is just a dream now. Oh, it was so lovely. My feet are swelling up something awful," said Anne with a half a smile. "And these sandals are brand new. I should've worn the shoes with the thick laces that I use for work. When I wear them, my feet don't swell." Anne frowned.

"Rest a minute. I have to tell you my news. My big event is coming up. My parents are planning a splash for my twenty-first birthday on October 31st. I'm the Halloween kid as you know. You and Josh are invited, and you'll be receiving an invitation soon. I've decided on a costume party, so start planning your getup."

"Really, oh my God, Josh and I will have to get a costume made. I'll get my Emily to design something. Her side business in designing clothes is growing. She's quite the artist. Did I tell you that Jim passed the courses and has become a manager and is selling loads of Ford cars? Their finances have improved, thank God. It was a worry, them buying that house outside of London. Meeting the mortgage payment each month was tough, but it looks like it's working out. We could come to your party as a famous couple. Hey, we could dress up as Duke and Duchess of Windsor? What a laugh we'll have. I'll have to get a wig and go on a diet. The duchess was very thin."

"My, that's a quick decision; now I won't be surprised."

"Oh, sorry, but you'd recognize us, wouldn't you? I can think of something else, but Matilda and her love of the royal family makes me think she'd like that. She's got us all involved in them. The royals were always her hobby. She filled a scrapbook of the whole lot. It would give her a big laugh to send pictures of us in a costume."

"Anne, I'm fine with your choice. Don't change your idea."

"Have you decided on your costume?"

"No. That will take me forever, but even if I knew, I wouldn't tell you."

"You're right not to. I've a big mouth and could never keep that secret. I can't ruin all the fun."

"What's the latest news?"

"Matilda has started her last class. When she is through with that she'll do her student teaching. For a while I thought her education was done with. Eric has sent the money for her to finish up. He told me this last week. I thought she was taking out loans. He's saved her. Eric's a good son. She's told him she'll pay him back once she finds a teaching position. I was so surprised. I had no idea he was still doing that. I planned to help her if she got stuck. Matilda never wanted to take any money from Mark. We always said she wants to be independent, but that's hard."

"I know you did. It's great she's finishing up. I'm still trying to decide when I'll return to business school, but I suppose I'll wait a while now."

"Get your strength back first. Okay, I'm ready to move on and explore the park. My feet feel better. I picked up a catalog. That open air theatre is playing a Shakespeare play today. It's too bad we can't make it. We'll have to do it some other time. What do you want to do? Queen Mary's Garden has 12,000 roses. I wonder if they're still in bloom. Do you want to go have a look? I just want to take a whiff," said Anne, slipping on her sandals.

"Of course I do," said Carrie.

"Good. Then after that we can take the Bird Walk. I could spend hours here. I'm getting hungry for something. A Dairy Ice would quench my thirst. Do you want one?"

"I do," said Carrie.

The two strolled onward, talking and laughing until they reached the stand where they sold cold refreshments. Anne purchased two ices "Wow, these are delicious," said Carrie. Meandering along, they spoke back and forth, enjoying the day and the highlights of Regent's Park.

Twenty-Two

A Surprise

Richard Evergreen walked into his computer company in Twinsburg and opened his office door. His green short sleeve shirt and print blue tie matched his easy manner, and the fresh marigolds sitting in a glass vase on his desk with a note beside it had Richard feeling ready for the day. He picked up the message from his employees, smiled, then put it down. Sorting through the papers on his desk, he stopped and looked up to see Donald Blair, his manager, holding the mail. Donald's broad hands just managed to keep the letters from falling.

"Those flowers are a welcoming sight. That's a nice welcome back. I'll thank the staff later. What have you got there? Looks like lots of mail," said Richard.

"It sure piled up."

"I better get busy," said Richard with a grin.

"You do. How was the trip to London?"

"I'd say it was successful, and I have you to thank for keeping the business running. Thank you."

"I'm glad you're satisfied. You seem so changed. Whatever you have, I'd like some of it," said Donald, remembering how somber Richard had been before he left for his vacation, and hoped he was over the car wreck which had set him back.

"Thanks, I'm better. Okay, I need to begin to catch up. I'd like you to continue to take all phone messages while I work through this, and tell the callers I'll get back to them at the end of the day."

"Right, will do," said Donald, leaving the office.

Richard had hired Donald Blair for his knowledge of technology and computers. Donald kept the customers happy, and had initiated the idea that it would save customers money if they brought their computer in to get repaired rather than putting out their money on a newer one. He advised Richard what he thought were the best computers on the market and looked through catalogues when sales people brought them to the store. He helped Richard with decision making, so Richard had begun to depend more and more on Donald.

Richard had started his business against the advice of his parents. They had said a small business could fall apart in a year, but his wife Sarah had encouraged him and often worked beside him. It was a few months after its opening when Sarah had died of an aneurism, but even with the deep loss of his wife, he had made the business work, and showed a profit.

Richard had refused to work for the Rosen family at the Skylight Inn, for he had no interest in the hotel business. Tinkering with computers for years, he knew this was what he desired as his life's work. But now he pondered about calling his parents with a phone call he knew would fill them with shock or surprise. With September here, his mother had said she would fly in and help him do back to school shopping. Richard knew she was waiting for his call. The Evergreens owned a local flower shop in Hollywood, California which kept them busy.

Richard stared at the phone, picked it up, and then put it back on the receiver. Then he thought he could email his parents. He returned to his work, but could not concentrate. "Damn, what can I tell them?" he asked himself. "How can I tell them that Matilda is getting a divorce, and I'm the reason for the breakup?"

He put down the papers and left the office for the coffee machine. Pouring himself a mug of black coffee, he tried to clear his mind. Back in the office, he picked up the ringing phone.

"A call for you, Richard," said the receptionist.

"I told Donald no calls until later."

"I know, but this is your mother calling from Hollywood, California. She said it's six-thirty a.m. and knew you would be at the office, and wanted to catch you before she started her day and you got too busy." Richard stared at his watch and saw it was already nine-thirty.

"Okay, connect us."

"Sure thing, Richard," said the receptionist. He pushed a button on his phone and heard his mother speak.

"Richard, dear, how are you. I was worried. How come I haven't heard a word since you returned from London?"

Richard swallowed hard. "Mom, so much has been going on. Sorry for not calling."

"I forgive you," she said. Richard being her only child, she constantly advised him on the management of his children. As he was a single father, he was often in a stew on how to raise them, and would call his mother for advice.

"How are Jennie and Joey doing? Have you booked a flight for me to come to Twinsburg?"

"No Mom, that won't be necessary."

"It won't?"

"Mom, are you sitting or standing?"

Sue gasped at that remark. "Richard, what's wrong?" she asked, feeling her stomach tighten.

"Nothing. Mom. Sit down and I'll explain."

"Okay, shoot. I'm listening."

"Mom, it's about Matilda."

"Matilda?"

"She's here in Twinsburg and taking her final courses at Kent

State University before student teaching And one more thing, she's separated from Mark Rosen and seeking a divorce."

"What? Did I hear right?"

"Mom, Matilda and I are to be married once the divorce is final."

"Oh my God," said Sue. "What did you say?"

"I said we'll be getting married."

"I'll call you back," said Sue. Richard heard the phone click.

* * * * *

Sue Evergreen wrapped her robe around her and shuddered. "My God, what has Richard done? This can't be," she said. "Oh my, the Rosen's. What will they say when they hear this? How can I ever go to Miami Beach at Hanukkah and Christmas vacation and spend time with our grandchildren there? No, no."

She sat there, staring at the wall while a thousand things flashed through her mind. "How can I tell Al this?" she said, hearing him singing in the shower. They had lots of orders to fill. There were celebrations coming up for the fall season which meant she would be preparing many elaborate arrangements. No matter how busy the shop was, she managed to take a trip to Twinsburg in the spring and autumn to spend time with her grandchildren. Shopping for back to school items and spending time with them was important to her.

"Sue," called Al. "I'm done. It's your turn. Hurry up, we have a busy day," said Al, leaving the bathroom and going upstairs.

"Okay," said Sue, entering the bathroom. With the water splashing over her back, she tried to think of the right words to tell her husband, but her mind froze.

"Oh my God, what do I tell him? Matilda is precious, and I always told Janet Rosen that I thought the world of her, and I still do. But her divorcing Mark Rosen and planning to marry Richard, can't be possible."

"Sue, what are you doing in there? Hurry up, we have to get

through that traffic and open up the shop. All those orders are waiting."

Out of the shower, Sue dried herself with a large bath towel then wrapped it around herself. "I'll be out in a jiffy," she called. "I'll tell him sometime today," she said, talking to her mirror, "but not now." She opened the door "Hello, dear. I'll dress fast, and we'll be on our way before you finish your morning coffee."

"Good, you're taking a long time," said Al, pacing up and down.

"I guess I'm slow today," said Sue, gathering up her makeup kit. "I'll be out of here in a minute."

"Good," said Al, returning to the kitchen to finish his coffee and check the morning newspaper sport's section for the golf tournaments, which he liked to attend when he could. Golf was an important part of his life. He put the paper aside.

"Ready?" he called up the stairs. "What's happening?"

"I'm all set."

"Well, you look gorgeous this morning," said Al. "And that rose clip in your hair will make our customers happy. They'll see that and want bunches of fresh roses."

"I put it on to give me a lift today. Glad you approve," said Sue.

Al picked up the car keys. "It's gonna be a hot one."

"I know."

Al gave a quick look around the house. Sue came out and followed Al to the car. Al pulled out of the driveway on to the highway of speeding cars.

"It's going to be a long day," thought Sue as she turned to look at her husband. She was about to utter something to him but changed her mind.

Twenty Three

A Shock

Ron Rosen phoned the temporary service and arranged for a replacement for Hilda. He glanced into the office and saw Hilda working on the computer. She looked up when Ron entered her office whistling.

"Good morning, Hilda," said Ron. "How are things going?"

"Hey, you surprised me. What's with the whistle? Something new in your repertoire?"

"You might say that, but here's the good news. Miss Clair Paley will be here in about ten minutes. She's your stand-in for the next two weeks, so you can take off on your vacation. I'm told she learns fast."

"Stand-in? I didn't know I was an actress," laughed Hilda. "Where did you find her?"

"Easy, she majored in business a few miles away at the University of Miami, and she knows her stuff, according to the temp service. She recently graduated and is looking for a job."

"Is that so? Great," said Hilda picking up her bottle of water and taking a sip. "I have to go to the bathroom and freshen up."

"Okay," said Ron, strolling back to his office. On his desk sat the invoices. He began looking through them while he listened for the bell door to ring. Hearing a light tap on the front door of the building, he hurried to open it. There stood a young girl with shoulder length brown hair, around five-feet six, wearing multi colored heels, and a big smile.

"Hi, I'm from the agency. I'm Clair Paley."

"Come on in, young lady. I was waiting for you. Follow me. I'm Ron Rosen." He took her to meet Hilda.

"Hilda," said Ron, opening the door. "I'd like you to meet Clair. She's going to help us."

Entering the office, Hilda looked at Clair approvingly. "Welcome to the Skylight Inn," said Hilda, sounding relieved.

"Okay, if you need me for anything, I'll be in my office," said Ron.

Sitting at his desk, he then phoned Janet.

"Hello, the Rose Restaurant. Janet speaking."

"Clair is here from that agency, and I have a feeling it'll work out. This girl looks real smart."

"Well, that's great. When did Hilda say she'd take off?'

"I don't know, but it'll probably be when she thinks that Clair knows the ropes."

"Okay, sounds good."

"What's happening over there?"

"It's busy, and we're short due to that virus. I'll have to make some calls to get some more help for today."

"What's Jay doing?"

"He's at the front desk today. He's doing a good job. He hasn't gambled for a good while. I hope he doesn't fall off the wagon. It's great seeing him like this. Okay, I'm sure to find someone to come in. I'll make the calls," said Janet.

"Okay, I have to get through some paper work, and then I'll come over."

Ron hung up the phone and continued working. After two hours, Hilda came out of her room with Clair and knocked on Ron's door.

"Ron," said Hilda, "I believe by the end of the day, Clair here will have a good idea of how we run things." Clair stood still with an air of confidence as her eyes focused on Ron.

"That's what I like to hear," said Ron, beaming.

They left his office, and Ron worked another four hours. "I need a bite," he said. Entering Hilda's office, he tried to speak to her, but she was busy showing Clair how the invoices worked, how to file information on the computer, and the names of the important clients that he needed to keep his business running. He waved at Hilda and pointed to the door. She acknowledged him and waved back.

"Let's see what's happening at The Rose. I'm hungry," he said to himself.

When he arrived, he saw Janet busily handing out menus. She didn't notice him enter. He sat down and picked up a menu Mary approached.

"Hi Mary. What are you doing here today? You're supposed to be running Sarah's Garden."

"Janet called and asked me to come over. More are out with that virus."

"It's that bad?"

"Seems like it."

"Well, don't you get it," chuckled Ron, studying the menu. He ordered a fish sandwich and looked up to see Janet coming over.

"It's bad, we might have to close up early, Ron."

"It is? Well, we aren't closing for a virus."

"How do we run it with half the staff out?" said Janet, her hands on her hips.

"Never give up. That's my motto. I took that line from Winston Churchill, the prime minister of England, the greatest leader of World War Two, and I've tried to live by that quote of his."

"It's good you have, Ron; but this is not a war. It's a bug."

"Right," said Ron, looking around. Mary brought him a mug of coffee, and it wasn't long before he finished eating. He pulled back his chair, ready to help run The Rose. Glancing across the room at his wife, he noticed she looked angry, and her eyes held a wild fiery glare. She was listening on the phone. Then it appeared to him she was about to crumble and faint. In an instant, Ron was beside her.

"What's the matter?" he asked, putting his arm around her. "Who was on the phone?"

"It was Sue Evergreen," she answered in a weak voice.

"Sue called? What's the matter? Are our grandchildren all right?"

"It's Richard and Matilda, that's what's wrong. Take me home. I can hardly stand up," said Janet in a muffled voice.

"Hold on to me," said Ron. Mary looked across the room and noticed something amiss. She thought Janet was about to throw up. Hastily, she put down the coffee pot and went to her. She turned her around.

"Mrs. Rosen, are you all right?" she asked.

"Mary, you'll have to do everything. I don't feel well."

"I'm sorry, Janet. Looks like you've gotten that bug. Let me help you to the door."

"Feel better," said Mary, pushing the door wide open. "It'll be all right here. I'll take care of things. You get some rest," she said, shaken at Janet's anguished face.

Ron escorted Janet to the house where she collapsed on the sofa. He went to the bathroom and brought a soaked washcloth, placed it on her forehead, then handed her a glass of cold water. She drank it and lay back on the pillow. Ron sponged her face.

"I just can't believe it. I can't," said Janet.

"What can't you believe?"

"It's Matilda. She's left Mark for Richard, our son-in-law."

"What? So that's why Mark couldn't tell us the reason for the separation. I must go to him."

"What can you do?"

"I don't know."

"Oh, I hate her more than ever."

"Stop that kind of talk, Janet. There's nothing we can do." He loosened his tie. "Are you all right now?"

"No!"

"Rest, I'll be back. I have to see Mark. I have to help him. Try to calm yourself. I'll be back a soon as I can." He left Janet drinking the water, looking as though her life was over. Ron rushed to Mark's office. His hands perspired. He knocked on the door and entered.

"Hi dad, what brings you here?"

"I stopped by to talk. Can you stop what you're doing and walk with me for a few minutes?"

"Whew, not right now. I've too much to do."

Ron glanced over at the new accounts assistant. "I can see you're doing okay here."

"Yes, I am; nice to meet you Mr. Rosen. I'm Paul Weaver."

"Welcome to the Skylight Inn. Sorry I haven't gotten over to meet you. I'm glad Mark has you here. Come on, Mark, let's go."

They walked to a bench that overlooked the gardens. Ron sat down. "Dad, you said you wanted to talk."

"Sit down, Mark. How are you feeling these days?"

"Dad, I'm okay now. I almost messed up the whole works when I was out of the office for so long. I'm sorry dad. I did have the accounts going so well, and then the separation from Matilda almost finished me. Paul knows the system now, so I'll be on my way soon. There are some job opportunities I'm thinking over."

"Mark, don't say another word about leaving us. Sue Evergreen phoned your mother a little while ago and told us everything that's been going on with you and Matilda. Listen, you'll be fine. You'll get over it. I want you to know we understand. Don't leave. We need you. I don't want to hear about you seeking another position."

Mark stared at his father. Trying to control his shaking hands, he buried his face in his hands and wept.

"Mark, life goes on," said Ron, putting his arm around his son's shoulders. "You'll heal from this. Come on, son. Come to the house. We'll talk."

Mark looked up at his father. "Dad, I just couldn't tell you. I feel so empty," he choked. "I just can't understand any of it."

"It's not you, Mark. It's what happens. The Skylight Inn can wait. Come home, and I'll make you the best omelet you ever tasted. I'm good at making those."

Mark wiped his eyes; they walked toward the house. The sun's rays gleamed on the palm trees, and a gentle breeze brushed over them. Reaching the front door of the Rosen household, Ron opened the front door. He hesitated and glanced upward, and saw a pelican flying alone.

"Look, Mark, at that pelican," said Ron. "Its wings are spread wide and firm. How graceful it flies. You'll be all right, son. Trust me."

Twenty-Four

The Birthday

The 31st of October had arrived. Carrie had left London after work and traveled to her parents' home. She awoke early and had a dream which she tried to recall. She had been some place with Matilda, but where it was she could not remember. Out of bed, she stretched her arms and legs and went to the window.

"Oh, lovely," she said, looking at the trees, grass, and flowers that surrounded the house. "What a lovely day for my birthday. Oh, I can't believe I'm twenty-one." Lingering there a while, she turned from the window to a soft knock on her door.

"Can I come in?" asked her mother. The door opened. "Happy Birthday, Carrie," she said, giving her daughter a warm hug. "So glad you're well. It's going to be a busy day. The caterers will be coming this morning to plan out everything. I'm so excited. I talked to a local band to come here. It's a good group of musicians; they'll be here around seven this evening. I gave them your favorite songs and some of mine to play. Want some breakfast?"

"No, not right now. I thought I'd take Oscar for a walk. Is dad around?"

"No, he went for an early spin on his bike."

"Okay then. I'll get dressed and check out the countryside."

"Go ahead. It's a lovely morning."

"Thanks for getting a band, Mom."

Carrie dressed. "Come on Oscar, let's go." Her dog bounded

toward her, and she put on his collar and attached the leash.

On a hill, Carrie gathered wild flowers, immersing her face in their scent. Strolling onward, she thought of Matilda who had phoned earlier to send her birthday greetings. She would have liked to share her birthday with her best friend, but knew that could not happen. Walking and thinking for an hour, she headed back to the house to find her mother standing by the front door.

"Oh, I'm so relieved you're back. I was coming to find you. The thick woods out there can be treacherous. The pathways wind on and on. We had a boy of seven lost there not too long ago, and the whole community was in an uproar, searching. They found him late at night sleeping with his dog next to him. I ran to warn you about the wood's density, but you disappeared. If you hadn't gotten back so fast, I'd be calling the police."

"Mum, that had to be awful about that boy, but I'm not stupid enough to walk in those woods alone; and I don't have my thick soled shoes on to tramp though loose branches. Oscar was with me. I would bet he knows his way around here."

"True, he does, but whether he could lead you back, I can't say. I'm relieved you didn't go far. Let me catch my breath. I have to sit down for a bit." After a few minutes, Rita got up. "Okay, I suppose I'm sane now. Are you ready for breakfast?"

"Yep, I am."

"Good, I'll make the tea."

"Is there anything you need help with?" asked Carrie as she unfastened Oscar's leash.

"Yes, you can help with setting the table." Opening the kitchen drawers, Carrie happily put out the knives, forks, napkins and glasses.

Carrie ate a breakfast of scrambled eggs, bacon, and a glass of chocolate milk. With breakfast over, she ran upstairs and pulled out her costume. She had planned to dress up as a famous English queen, but decided on Cleopatra, ruler of Egypt who was feared, respected, and powerful, which Carrie often said she would like to emulate. She thought of Cleopatra as a great woman of her time. Holding the costume up to her neck, Carrie smiled at her reflection in the mirror.

"Yes, yes, it's gorgeous," she said, slipping the costume and black wig back into the wardrobe.

Downstairs, Carrie heard voices and the clatter of pots and pans. She rushed down.

"Can I do something?"

"No," said the head cook. "You must be the birthday girl."

"I am."

"In that case love, you are queen for the day."

"I am," laughed Carrie. "I really am."

All the guests arrived at five o'clock. Carrie and her parents greeted them and complimented the guests on their costumes. There was only one man who arrived in a gray business suit, white shirt, and a light blue tie.

"Hello, I don't believe we've met," said Carrie.

"Good evening, Cleopatra," said the man. "I'm a friend of your parents who graciously invited me to your celebration. I, too, am an admirer of Cleopatra and Caesar."

"Great," said Carrie. "Welcome."

The guests mingled. Carrie opened her presents and beamed while the band played her favorite songs. She smiled and laughed at Brian who was dressed as Charlie Chaplin. He threw his walking stick in the air and caught it, then imitated the trade walk Chaplin used in his silent films.

"Oh, your costumes are marvelous," said Carrie, smiling at everyone. "Thank you all for coming to celebrate my twenty-first." She looked at her father who was pushing through the group along with the gentleman she did not know.

106

"Okay, get your phones ready to take pictures." said Carrie's mother. "It's time to cut the birthday cake."

Carrie's eyes glowed as she listened to her family and friends sing Happy Birthday. Blowing out the candles in one breath, Carrie made the traditional wish one makes at becoming of age, which meant she was independent to make her own choices. "I'm officially an adult now," she said grinning. At this statement her friends clapped and cheered.

"They've good lungs, Carrie," said her father, giving her a big hug. He then introduced the guest who had come without a costume. "Carrie, this is David Patterson, an inheritance lawyer. He has something to present to you."

"Ah, what?" said Carrie.

"Hello, Carrie I have an announcement," said the lawyer. "I have this will. It states when becoming twenty-one you will receive an inherited sum of money from your grandmother, to be given to you on that day. Here it is, but first I have to read all that has been requested from your beloved late grandmother. Ready?"

"Oh, my God," uttered Carrie, holding onto her father. "No, this can't be true. An inheritance I have an inheritance?"

"Yes, you have, and I have to give you the name of your financial advisor. He's Robert Macintosh, who will be guiding you. This is a request from your grandmother, that you contact him as early as possible. Here is his business card," said Mr. Patterson.

"Oh, this can't be!" she said.

"It is," said Mr. Patterson, with a grin. "Come, I have so much to explain to you."

"Excuse us for a little while," said Gary to the guests. "We have to talk."

The party goers remained quiet, then clapped. Carrie looked dazed enough to make her family and friends think she was about to faint. Pulling herself together, she entered the kitchen with her parents and the lawyer. Carrie sat at the kitchen table looking bewildered. Outside the door, her guests drank champagne and sang "For she's a jolly good fellow," with the band playing and singing along.

Twenty-five

The Inheritance

A breeze coming from the open window awakened Carrie. She threw off the wool blankets and closed the bedroom window. Opening a drawer from the night stand, she pulled out the will and read again the details of her inheritance. Unable to sleep until the early hours of the morning, she yawned, staring at the formal paper stating the amount of money she had inherited.

"Oh, my God, one hundred thousand pounds," she called out. "Can this be?" She fell on the bed and rolled over and over. "I can do whatever I want," she squealed. "Oh, but I can't touch the money for two months. Damn!"

The clock radio alarm blasted out music. Carrie shut it off. Grabbing her dressing gown she headed downstairs. Her mother was in the kitchen turning on the cold water tap.

"How's the party girl this morning, or should I say the heiress?"

"Mum, I'm sort of bewildered. Don't you think it's amazing that grandmother left money to me?"

"From what I know, some grandparents do that, but she wanted you to do some planning. Mr. Mackintosh will be your financial guide, so take heed and listen to him."

"That's right he will. Darn, his name sounds like a rain storm, and he's probably so dull. And I know he'll lecture me," said Carrie in a whiney voice.

"Cone on, Carrie, you had better make a phone call to meet him.

I don't know about the dull part, but remember, he'll be doing his job, according to the will."

The door opened and Gary came in. "How did you enjoy your birthday party? Not bad eh? Your friends had a great time, and the best part was your inheritance."

"Dad, to think your mother left me all that money."

"She certainly did, and she made sure that you don't spend it too fast. I had one smart mother. We'll be mailing a check to your brother Larry, too. As he's older, he has no stipulations. You ought to travel to see him."

"I will one of these days, but I could use the money right now."

"From what has been written and stated, you can't touch a penny for two months. You'll work it out I'm sure," said Gary.

Carrie stared at him and reached up to hug him. "Dad, you're right. I'm just so overwhelmed."

"You two ready to eat something? Come and sit down, and have something," said Rita.

Stirring her tea, Rita smiled. "I'd say the fancy dress costume party was a hit. We've taken loads of pictures. Your friend Shania sang my favorite song. She's terrific, and Brian dressed as Charlie Chaplin was plain magic. It's good he could make it. I got a member of the band to make a video because he knows someone that's good at editing, so we can send one to Matilda if you want."

"Matilda, oh, won't she be surprised when I tell her my news, and I'll be able to visit her very soon. She'll love seeing her mother and Josh dressed as the Windsor's. I'll never have a better party than that. I better get moving. I have to catch the early the train to London. It's work tomorrow. I'll borrow a big bag, Mum, to take back my presents."

"Not so fast, Carrie, first you have to contact Mr. Mackintosh to arrange how to work out your finances, and then locate a bank to deposit your inheritance. This takes planning, so I'll go with you to London Monday morning."

"Oh, my God, I'll call Yamsing's and take a personal day. It's Sunday. What was I thinking? No one will be there. I'll leave a message with Frank Evans, my manager. He's so cool."

"Good, I'll put everything important in my old briefcase that I used in my law practice," said Gary.

"That's settled then," said Rita, getting up to wash the breakfast dishes.

"Well, daughter, how about taking a spin this morning? Helen of Troy is waiting. I've shined her up. You'll love buzzing past the river and through the county lanes. But I have to avoid the areas where milking cows graze. I don't want to make their milk sour. Come on, get dressed. I'll be in the garage."

"Gary, you and that darn bike, it's such a pain. Must she ride on the back? It's so dangerous."

"You bet I must, Mum. Remember, I'm officially an adult."

"I know."

Rita sighed as she dried the dishes. She looked over at Oscar waiting for a treat. Pleased she had kept the secret of Carrie's inheritance, she was nevertheless concerned.

"Well, we've done all we can to warn her of pitfalls. We can do no more." She stared at Oscar who begged for another treat. "No, Oscar, not now. I've been feeding you too much. You need a walk. Come on, let's get going." Oscar ran around the hallway in circles. "Stand still. I have to get your leash on. Okay? Ready? Good," said Rita, opening up the back door.

Twenty-Six

Carrie's Work

Carrie returned to her job. She did her best to calm herself, but the thought of her inheritance under her name in a bank, had her fumbling with documents piled up waiting to be looked over. Unable to concentrate, she got up and went to the fountain for a drink of water and bumped into Frank Evans holding some papers.

"Oh, there you are Carrie. I heard you just had a big birthday party. Becoming twenty-one is a milestone in your life. Happy Birthday, I was just coming over to talk to you."

"Oh, thank you for your good wishes," she said, sipping the water.

"How are you adjusting to being back at work? Are you feeling better?"

"I'm as good as new, Mr. Evans. I can do all that you ask. Is there something you need me to do right now?"

"Yes, there is. Let's go over to your desk."

Frank gave Carrie a printed handout to read. "Here, I want to ask you to help us raise funds for our charity we have each year. Yamzing's raises money for our Christmas fund to help families in need. We begin early by selling raffle tickets for the best seat in a theatre production in the West End. The winner will also meet the actors, have dinner in a fine restaurant, and receive household gifts from a department store on Oxford Street. I have the staff participate in this project, so we hope to sell lots of tickets. As you weren't here yesterday, you missed the meeting explaining our charity. We make sure that these families have the best Christmas we can give them."

"Of course, I'd be delighted," said Carrie.

"Good, the information is on this handout. We'd like them sold in the next couple of weeks. Okay?" He smiled at her. "Here are the tickets. I'll let you get back to work. I'll see you at lunch."

Carrie thoughtfully placed the raffle tickets on the corner of her desk, cleared her mind and began working. She liked Frank Evans. His manner and smile made her feel good. She remembered Regina saying what a good boss he was. Deep within her, she knew she wanted to get to know him, but felt it was impossible because he was her boss.

After working for three hours, the phone rang. Carrie picked it up.

"Hello, Yamzing's."

"Hi, this is Sabrina Zack from Brian Price's office. Please hold."

"Hi, Carrie, how's your day so far? I've been busy, but I'm ready for our lunch date. Do you want to go out of the building?"

"Brian, can you actually get a break?"

"Yep, I'll be over in an hour. Your party was great. I'm glad I made it, but this afternoon I'll be loaded again, so we'll try and stretch lunch today."

"Sounds okay. My dad laughed so hard at your Charlie Chaplin impersonation."

"He did?"

"Yeah. Okay, I'll see you soon."

Carrie hung up the phone feeling pleased that she could spend some time with Brian. She felt grateful for his guidance and help in learning her job. Then she began thinking about her future. Mr. Mackintosh had told her to expect him to see her once a week to show how to organize and manage her inheritance.

"Oh, this is all so ridiculous," she said out loud. "I'm not a child. I won't spend it all at once." She thought of the list she had scribbled of things she wanted. "Damn, Mr. Mackintosh will probably tell me no; and don't do this and don't do that." Putting her thoughts aside, she returned to concentrating on her work, hardly noticing the old clock above the lift had reached twelve o' clock. Brian approached her desk.

"Boo!" yelled Brian, tapping Carrie on her back.

"Oh, it's you, Brian. You scared me half to death. It must be lunch time."

"It is. Come on. Get your coat. We're walk by the River Thames and stop at one of those little luncheonettes. It's a bit windy, so take your scarf. I had a sandwich there last week and hot apple pie. It's the best. You can treat me now you're rich," laughed Brian.

"Brian, please don't say that, or anything to anyone about my inheritance."

"Of course I won't, but people do have ways of finding out everything. I'll keep my mouth closed," said Brian, putting two fingers to his lips. "I'm just joking. Look, it's my treat today."

"I can't touch a penny for two months, but it's a bit of shock getting this money and a lovely surprise, but it's not enough for me to stop working. Anyway, I can't talk about it."

"Okay, let's get going. Lunch hour is the fastest hour of the day."

"It is. You can tell me about your new position. Do you like it?"

"I do indeed. I've so much to learn, but it's what I've always wanted. The fashion show was tough to organize, and I was anxious the whole time. Lucky for me, we sold a lot of our new lines. Customers have been ordering since they saw the show. Yamzing's is going to have a good year if it continues like this."

"That's great. That means job security, right?"

"It certainly does."

114

They arrived at the luncheonette and found an empty table. "Are you ready for a great sandwich?"

"Am I? That bland diet for six weeks was bloody awful."

"Good. I'll order. Just tell me what sandwich you'd like"

"Something bad for me, spicy, hot, and delicious. Salami will do it."

"Okay, I'll wave to the waitress."

Twenty-Seven

An Encounter

Carrie gathered a towel, a bottle of liquid soap, some shampoo, and running shoes, then placed them in her gym bag. She had decided to exercise at the health club after a long day. First, she phoned Shania to ask her to join her, but said she couldn't go because of her voice training class. Then Carrie tried to contact Anne who often went with her to exercise, but all Carrie heard was the answering machine, so she left a message.

This last week, Carrie had often felt her stomach twinge. Wasn't coming into money supposed to make you feel content? Or was it because the list she had poured over trying to make decisions on what she would like to purchase made her feel so discombobulated.

She could still hear Mr. Mackintosh's voice groaning on through their last meeting. "Here is a budget that you should carefully follow," he had said, pointing out the mistakes she might make.

"You're being ridiculous!" she had said, then picked up her handbag and left, slamming the door so hard that loose papers flew off his desk. He had picked them up, shaking his head in dismay.

At the gym, she walked around the track for a mile and then got on a treadmill. Wiping down the machine with a clean towel she began to increase her speed. She was prepared to walk two miles. Looking at the machine beside her, to her astonishment, she saw Frank Evans grinning at her.

"Oh my God," she mumbled.

"Hello, Carrie. How you doing? I just joined the club; so you're a member, too! I've decided a walk around the City is not enough, so here I am. How do you like it here?"

"I like it. I usually come with a friend, but it seems I couldn't get anyone to join me this evening."

"Is that so? Well, it's good to see you. You're looking well. I'm going to try and make it here on a regular schedule. Exercise helps clear my mind after a long day."

"It does do that. I think I'll try the track now," she said, stopping.

"I'll join you," said Frank.

On the track, Carrie found it overflowing with people of all ages, moving and pacing to their needs. Frank slowed his pace. After a half hour Carrie stopped. "I've had enough for tonight," she said wiping her forehead with a towel.

"I'll call it quits too," said Frank. "How about having a cup of tea with me?"

"Tea? Where?" asked Carrie.

"Down the street there's a little café not far from the gym."

"Okay, I'll shower and meet you by the lobby in about fifteen minutes."

"Good," said Frank, smiling.

Showering, Carrie felt a sense of excitement about going to a café with her boss. Then she began questioning herself. *"One should not go out with one's boss It's wrong. But he saved my life! He's my hero. But I can't go."*

At the lobby, she met Frank. "Mr. Evans, thank you for the invitation, but I'm feeling tired. The workout was tough, so I'll have to say no to tea."

"Are you sure?"

"Yes, I need to get back."

"Okay, then. Can we do it another time?"

"Yes, another day will be fine."

Carrie got on the bus knowing that Frank Evans was someone she wanted in her life. She felt attracted to his smile and the kindness he gave to all employees.

Arriving home and yawning, she opened up her mail box and picked up her mail along with a postcard with a picture of the Rock and Roll Hall of Fame in Cleveland, Ohio. Carrie squealed. "It's Matilda. She's sent me another postcard! Oh, I have to see the rock stars."

Opening her front door, she switched on the lights. Kicking off her shoes, she rushed into the kitchen and read her friend's card. It stated her divorce would be over in December and she would possibly marry sometime in January, or she might wait until spring when her student teaching was complete. In heavy print Matilda had written: "Carrie, I need you to come to my wedding. It will be in the town hall with a small reception following, but I can't imagine getting married without you, my mother, and family attending. Please say you'll come?"

Carrie stared at the postcard, then laughed. "Of course I can go. Well, I hope I can. I'll be rich soon. I'll phone her and tell her I'll plan to, but it will depend on me having the money. Oh, I'm sure I can get my inheritance early."

She walked over to Pete. "I hope you weren't too lonely today," she said, opening the cage. "Sorry I'm late." Her budgie pecked her cheek and then flew around the room, finally diving on her head. "I better shop tomorrow." Finding the peanut butter, she made a sandwich. "Okay, little one, I'll feed you," she said, popping Pete back in the cage.

Twenty-Eight

A Contract

Shania Della rushed to the phone. She was about to leave for work after swallowing some cereal, a slice of toast, and a cup of coffee. "I've got it. I've got it," she called out, grabbing the phone. Listening to the voice, her stomach flipped. Her mother entered, curious to learn who had called so early in the morning.

"What's going on? Who's on the phone?" she asked, washing maple syrup from her hands, having indulged in blueberry pancakes, her favorite breakfast, which Shania had refused.

"Mum, it was the manager from the Palm Jazz Club. He said to come in and sign a contract for a longer stay."

"He did, baby? Well, that's just grand. Heck, I knew you didn't have to worry one little bit. I saw his face after you sang."

"You did? I have to sign the contract tomorrow morning. I'll tell them at work today. Oh, I'm so excited."

"Wonderful, baby. Do you want me to go with you to the club?"

"Sure I do. I have to run. I have a client coming in early. Oh, I can't wait to tell everyone," she said to her beaming mother.

"I just knew you'd get a contract. It's no fluke. You've been working hard for this break. I'll make some phone calls. Just about everyone I know will want to see you perform."

Shania flew out of the house, but came back. "Mum, I forgot my handbag," she said, running over to the bookcase to retrieve it.

"Shania, calm down," called her mother as the front door shut.

Arriving at the shop, Shania told her manager the news.

"Are you saying you won't continue working here?"

"Oh, no, of course not," said Shania. "I'll continue to be a manicurist in the day, but I'll be singing in the club at night, so you'll all have to come and cheer me on." The beauticians laughed and got back to their chairs and their waiting clients who bent their ears to listen.

Carrie was sitting at her desk at Yamzing's when she received a phone call from Shania.

"Shania, that's the best news I've heard today. Do you want me to go shopping with you to find a gown?"

"Yes. I'd like that."

"Okay, let me know when." Carrie hung up the phone and began thinking about Matilda's upcoming wedding.

"My money, I haven't any. How can I go anywhere until the two months are up? Oh, there has to be some way." And then she knew. She would convince Mr. Mackintosh she must attend her friend's wedding, and the two months would be up by the time she made plans to leave. "I must convince him," she said, fumbling for a pen in the desk drawer.

Across the room, Regina waved. Carrie waved back. Looking down, she saw the raffle tickets sticking out at the corner of her desk.

"Damn, I forgot about them," she said, shoving them in her handbag. "Who do I sell them to now?" she moaned, then knew. "My first visit will be to Anne and Josh. They'll help me. Anne knows lots of people at Charlene's, and Josh knows tons of people where he works."

Carrie returned to her work, but could not concentrate, so decided to take her first brief morning break. Regina arose from her desk.

"Hi, Carrie," she said. "Are you ready for a snack? You look as though you could use a break. Is everything all right?'

"Oh, it's just the usual things. My mind seems bogged down today. Something decadent would be just the thing to pick me up this morning, like a fat chocolate doughnut."

Regina laughed. "Okay, let's go to the cafeteria. There was a meeting last night, and I heard there are some delicious pastries left over."

"Sounds exactly what I need. I'm just about out of everything at home. I must grocery shop tonight."

"Fine, let's go," said Regina.

Twenty-Nine

The Decision

Mark Rosen blinked while looking at his passport picture and tucked it in his desk. Studying the brochures scattered on the bed, he tried to determine where to go. Whether to take a trip around the world or visit just one country cluttered his mind. He had flipped through the bright pamphlets, staring at China, Spain, France, Italy, and Africa, scrawling at the top of his list. Usually, he could easily make fast decisions, but not this time.

Having spent most of his years working, with few breaks from the hotel, he had thought just maybe he could get away. He decided a vacation was needed if he was ever going to recover from the divorce. Soon he would sign the final papers. He had married Matilda on Christmas Eve, and during the night he thought of his wedding day, and had lain awake. It was then he'd made his decision to leave before Christmas Eve and voyage somewhere far from the Skylight Inn. At five a.m. he dressed. Choosing his old blue denim jacket, comfortable jeans, and tennis shoes, he took off. Along the beach, a few joggers zigzagged past him. His thoughts were with his father who he intended to meet for breakfast at The Rose and announce his plans.

Finishing his walk, he ventured to The Rose. Mark sat and waited. Glancing at the headlines of the morning newspaper, he frowned and put the newspaper aside. It was then he saw his father approaching.

"Morning, Mark, I'm real hungry. You okay? Did you order

anything yet? I think Goldie is working the early shift. She's good for the morning. Her smile lights up the place like Christmas tree lights. We need a big tree in the foyer. Before you know it, we'll have to get the Skylight Inn ready for the holidays. Goldie's going to see her family. She said her dad's not too well. We'll miss her."

"Oh, that's too bad. We need her around here. Will she come back?"

"I don't know. So why do you want to see me so early?"

"Dad, it's time."

"Time? What do you mean by time? Are you going to leave us? I thought things were better now. I won't hear of it!"

"I'm taking off for a month or longer, to get away. You know, kick back a bit see another country and do something different. I'll be away the rest of December and part of January."

"What about Christmas and Hanukah? We have the Continental Circus coming and we need you to run it. You know, do the usual things that only you can. We'll have lots of tourists. Can't you go after the holidays?"

"Dad, I can't be here then. Don't you understand?"

Ron stared into his son's sad blue eyes. A downcast look covered Mark's face, and his body slumped.

"Okay, I'll get Aaron on board and introduce him to the accounts. That new man you hired, Paul Weaver, seems to be doing okay, right? Jay can help with the Continental Circus. He's doing better. I don't think he's gambled since he came back. Go for it, take a vacation. We'll have to manage. Here comes Goldie with the menu."

"Morning, Miss Dimples. I'm ready to order the full family breakfast. How are you this morning?"

"Fine, Mr. Rosen, I'll get the coffee. And you Mark, what can I bring you?" asked Goldie smiling.

"The same thing," said Mark, his eyes glued to the table.

"Fine," said Goldie, collecting the menus.

"Okay, son, so where do you think you'd like to go?"

"I'm getting closer on that. I'm thinking Spain. I'd like to see a bullfight. It's daring and gutsy. Ernest Hemingway's 'The Sun also Rises' left an impression on me. I soaked it up in college. Bullfighters fascinate me. If I decide on Spain, I'll tour Madrid and other famous spots. I'd like to check out the architecture and castles. I could bring back some information for Aaron. He still wants to become an architect. If I go there, I'll shoot the best spots for him to view."

"Yes, that's what Aaron wants when his internship is up. I shouldn't have pressed any of you to sign a contract to intern here, but I thought at the time it was a good idea. It kept you on task. It was important that you all learned how to run it. The Skylight Inn will be all of my sons' inheritance, but the majority will be yours. So you see, even if you do leave, this Skylight Inn will be mostly in your name, so consider that!"

"Dad, please don't say anything more, but it was the best idea to teach us how a hotel works. We've all learned lots."

"That's good for me to know. Before you leave, make amends with your mother."

"Dad, that's a sore pain right now, but I'll think on it."

Goldie came to the table with the breakfast that the tourists liked. "Here we are," said Goldie smiling.

"Looks good," said Ron. "Thank you, Goldie. We have the best chefs; and look at those lush strawberries. No wonder the tourists like our hotel."

"Oh, they do, Mr. Rosen. Everything here is just wonderful. I'll miss all of you."

"Well, Goldie, your job will be here whenever you choose to return."

"Thank you, Mr. Rosen. I don't want to leave, but I have to." Her friendly personality shone which made Mark grin with appreciation.

"We're going to miss her. Okay, Mark, I'll call a meeting with our staff and let them know you'll be going away. Let me know the date when you'll be off. I must say Spain looks grand."

Mark finished his food. "I think it'll be Spain. As soon as I sign the divorce papers, I'll be off."

They stood up. Ron put his arm around Mark. "Have a good time, Mark. You deserve it. Come back rested."

"Thanks, dad," said Mark, holding a linen napkin over his mouth to prevent him from sobbing.

Thirty

The Advisors

Carrie phoned Mr. Mackintosh requesting if she could touch her inheritance a month earlier, and he immediately said no. He stated she could begin to draw money from her account January 1st and not a day before in accordance with her grandmother's will.

Disappointed, Carrie phoned her father and asked for a loan to attend Matilda's wedding. He said no. He decided his daughter must learn the value of what his late mother was trying to teach her, and the biggest lesson, he thought, was patience. Carrie then phoned Anne and asked if she could stop by and visit during the week. It was on a Wednesday evening Carrie took off to Anne's flat.

Anne opened the door and hugged Carrie. Nifty greeted her and swung around her legs while Carrie knelt down to pet him "You're still the cutest black and white cat I've ever seen."

"So what have you been up to this past week?" asked Anne, filling up the kettle with cold water. "What's the matter? I see a worried look written all over your face. Sit down and have a cupper. I have those chocolate biscuits you like, providing Josh didn't finish the bloody lot."

Carrie blew her nose with a tissue. "Oh, that would be lovely."

The kettle boiled and Anne poured the water into her china teapot and let the tea leaves brew.

"Here we go; have a biscuit. Have two," she said, giving Carrie a flowered English bone china cup and saucer she had inherited from her mother which she filled with strong tea.

Carrie dipped a biscuit into her tea. "Ooh, one could die for these."

Anne chuckled. "I know. So, do you want to tell me what's wrong?'

Carrie nodded and proceeded to tell Anne she would not be able to attend the wedding if it was held in January.

"Carrie, don't worry about that, the latest news is it'll be in the spring, not January. Matilda has to finish up with student teaching. After that, she'll receive her degree. She said they plan to marry in the town hall in the spring with a small reception following. I'm not certain that I'll be going, and the date could change again.

I'm not ready for another long trip, and Matilda mentioned they all might come here in the summer. Look, in two months you'll be able to use your inheritance, so you can visit Matilda anytime you want. You have mentioned going back to school. I believe it is your best decision yet. Flittering away your time is not the best thing. Is it?"

"True. Anne, you're sounding like Mr. Macintosh. Most of all, I want to travel before I end up sitting in a wheelchair and too old to go places. Seeing the world as much as I can, appeals to me. I want to learn about other cultures."

"Well, if that's what you want to do, go for it. I think I better stay out of any decisions. I'm not so good at giving advice."

"But you're right about school. I'll eventually do that. I'm impressed that Matilda is getting her university degree."

"We are all thrilled to."

Carrie opened her bag and pulled out the raffle tickets. "Anne, I have these raffle tickets. Could you help sell a few? Yamzing's is raising funds for the less fortunate families for Christmas, and I haven't sold one ticket. I forgot to take them home and left them on my desk, so I'm behind. I know you work with lots of people, and my boss Frank Evans has been so good to me. I just can't let him down with not selling any."

"I see a twinkle in your eyes. He's the one that took you to the hospital. Do you like him?"

"Of course I do. He's a good manager, and I respect him. He asked me out for tea a few days ago, but I said no."

"You didn't go? Why? I think that was nice of him. Okay, hand over the raffle tickets. There are plenty of people I work with who would like a chance to see a West End show."

"Oh, good," said Carrie. "Could Josh take a few to his job?"

"I'll ask him when he comes home. He's working late tonight."

"Thank you, Anne. I appreciate it."

"You're welcome."

"I'd still like to visit Miami Beach again."

"You would?"

"Yes, I like it there. I can still see the ocean, the palm trees, and the sand. I could go on and on, and the best part is the luxurious Skylight Inn. One of these days, I'll go back."

"I understand, but you do know that there's flooding in the streets due to the ocean rising. Global warming has come there, which is such a shame. I read all about it. Our environment is a mess. Maybe you should think of somewhere else to go."

"Really, I had no idea! It's dreadful, but still my favorite place. I still want to go there."

"I know," said Anne, collecting the dishes and placing them in the kitchen sink.

"I'd like to make the wedding when Matilda does finally settle on the date." It was then Carrie could not contain her laughter. "Oh, Anne, please forgive me. Sorry, I didn't mean anything by my laughing. I'm acting stupid. It must be my nerves, but her wedding to

Mark was beautiful. It was plain spectacular."

"That's true. It was," said Anne, picking up Nifty. "And I hope this wedding, whenever it takes place, will be her final one. I just want her to be happy."

Calming herself, Carrie looked serious. "I'm sure it will be, Anne."

Thirty-One

Sue's Viewpoint

Sue Evergreen put the last bouquet of flowers on the counter and wrote out a greeting card. She picked up the phone to make a call, but changed her mind. "Al, is everything cleaned up back there? I'm tired and ready to go home. You have to deliver this last order. I'm gonna sit down and rest while you do that."

Al Evergreen came out of the back room. "Everything is okay. I've swept up, watered the plants, and picked up stuff. We did fine today."

"We have," said Sue "And the holidays will be with us before we turn around. What am I going to do about Miami Beach? That's when I take my annual trip to the Skylight Inn and Richard brings the grandchildren, but with all this chaos, it won't happen."

"No, of course not. Richard's the last person the Rosen's would ever wish to see again. I'm not bothered by the divorce. Why did you think I would be?"

"I was surprised how you accepted it. It's like the whole world turned upside down for me."

"Listen, those two belong together. I've always known it. I'll have to check with Richard again to get a definite date of the wedding before I get the plane reservations. You need to call him."

"I'm not doing that. Besides, I have no idea what to say to him."

"Now that's crazy. You've always had a million things to tell him, and now you can't speak to him. For God's sake, Sue, he's loved

Matilda for a long time. Life's too short to be so upset. Start shopping for a party dress because we're going to their wedding, and we're gonna stay a while and see a show at the Cleveland Playhouse Square and care for our grandchildren when Richard and Matilda take off on their honeymoon."

"When did you decide on all of this?"

"I've been talking to Richard all along because he knows how you feel about the divorce. Damn, he needs someone to comfort him, not destroy him. He almost died in that car wreck, and now he's well I want him to enjoy his life."

"What are you thinking? I'm just flabbergasted. I'm not sure if I'll go."

"Of course you will."

Sue got up. "How could you make these decisions to go to Twinsburg and not tell me?"

"I decided the best thing I could do for our son is to attend his wedding."

"I see," said Sue. "I'm so unsure about everything, but I want what's best for our son."

"Okay, that's good. Call him early in the morning, and let him know you'll be there for him."

"I'll think about it. I'm going to call Janet Rosen. I'm hoping she'll agree to have me visit during the holiday season, and if possible, have Richard send our grandchildren to the Skylight Inn. I know they plan to have the Continental Circus return to the Skylight Inn. Our grandchildren can't miss out on that. They went wild for the clowns. Remember how we promised Sarah we'd help teach the children both religions? Well, I intend to keep that promise. I'd like Janet to heal along with me. Besides, it's been a tradition. Since they were born, our families have met there. The children love going to the Skylight Inn and lighting the Hanukkah candles, decorating the Christmas tree and singing carols on Christmas Eve. They look forward to the two holidays. I must do this for them. Can't you see that?"

"Suit yourself. It'll be like opening up a can of worms talking to Janet."

"Well, I'll soon find out."

"I've heard enough. I'll deliver the flowers. I'll be back soon."

"All right, Al."

Sue opened the cash register and added up the sales for the day. Balancing up, she sat down. She thought of Matilda, and often commented on how she would have loved to have a daughter like her, but never dreamt it would happen like this. She saw Matilda's goodness. Sitting there, Sue's cheeks flushed. "I can do nothing about any of this," she said, standing up. "Al is right, but it'll be so hard. Oh, it's all so crazy and such a mess!"

Sue entered the bathroom and rinsed her face. Looking in the mirror, she felt pleased she had the plastic surgery which she did every few years. Sue had decided her appearance was important in her business, "Well," she sighed, "I better start looking for a dress for my son's wedding. Tomorrow, I'll contact Janet Rosen. Oh God, give me the guts and energy to do this," she mumbled as she located her jacket.

The door swung open. "The flowers are delivered dear, and I got the biggest thank you."

"You did? You got there and back fast. I'm ready," said Sue, zipping her jacket.

"Okay, I'll get the car."

"Good," said Sue, switching off the shop's lights and locking up. Satisfied, she joined Al.

"You okay?" he asked, looking up.

"I have to be," said Sue, buckling her seat belt.

"Great, it's the rush hour and time for calmness," said Al.

"True," said Sue, closing her eyes.

Al looked over at her. "It'll all work out. You'll see," he said in a soft voice.

Thirty-Two

Someone's Missing

Everyone at Yamzing's waited for Frank Evans to pick up the money for the sold raffle tickets. Carrie had placed the left over tickets and money in her desk drawer in an envelope.

Calmly, she began her day's work. For a moment she stopped to glance around the office to see if Frank was coming through the door. "Where is he?" she said out loud. It was then she saw Brian visiting the desks and talking to the employees. He held a brief case. "What's he doing here?" she asked herself.

Brian approached Carrie. "How are you on this gorgeous sunny morning?" he asked, propping the briefcase on her desk. "You look so pretty in that red dress and dangling earrings. Where did you get them? Were they at our fashion show? I can't recall all the items we showed."

"No, Brian. I treated myself at the Barnes store. What are you doing here so early?"

"I've come to pick up the money for the sold raffle tickets."

"Oh, so you're collecting." Carrie gave the envelope to Brian and signed a paper with the amount raised.

"Looks like you sold most of them," he said, looking over the contents.

"Lucky for me I did. I got some help."

"That's good. Looks like I won't make it for lunch today. I'll be busy collecting the spoils, and counting," laughed Brian.

"Why, where's Frank?"

"I don't know. He's responsible for lots of stuff around here, so he must be involved with something more important."

"I suppose he is," said Carrie, frowning.

"I'll see you tomorrow for lunch."

"Okay, Brian, we'll catch up then."

Carrie continued working. She felt her stomach tighten. She missed Frank's greeting and that special smile of his. "I wonder where he is," she asked herself as she kept looking toward the lift, hoping he would appear when the doors opened.

She completed the work. Looking around, she saw Regina and waved. "Ill pop over and talk to her," she said. Finding a loose rubber band in her desk drawer, she bound up the documents she had printed from her computer, put them in a neat pile, then walked over to Regina.

"Hello, I've caught up, but Mr. Evans is not around to inform me what else he wants done today, so I'm going for a bite and some coffee. Would you like to join me?'

"No, I can't go. I'm behind, and I didn't manage to sell many tickets. I feel bad about that," said Regina, facing the computer.

"Oh, I'm sorry. Do you know where our boss is?'

"No, I don't," she said, continuing to work "I'll give his secretary a buzz after I finish this. I'm so behind today, but I'll get in touch with Ruby and find out."

"Do you want me to bring you something back?" asked Carrie, looking about the room, waiting for the big old clock to chime on the hour, and hoping Frank might appear with his cheerful greeting.

"That would be nice, Carrie. A cup of coffee should do it and a pastry would be nice," said Regina, searching in her wallet for her money.

"Put that away. It's my treat today."

135

Regina yawned, putting her hand over her mouth. "Oh, excuse me. I should have gotten to bed earlier. I got involved last night with watching an old movie. Thank you."

Arriving at the cafeteria, Carrie queued up for a sandwich and coffee. She sat down and said hello to a man sitting there wearing blue work clothes with his sleeves rolled up. He had a brown smudge on his cheek. "Hello," she said, and introduced herself. "What do you do?'

"Allo, love. I'm Ted Brownstein. I'm the fixer upper around 'ere. There's always somethin' that needs me touch. The phone never stops blinkin' or ringin'," he said, dipping a biscuit into his mug of tea. "Sorry, me 'ands are grubby. I didn't get a chance to wash 'em. I've just got through a plumbin' problem. All that bloody rain flooded the lower level. But it's all back to normal now. You must be new 'ere. I 'aven't seen you about."

"I suppose I am. I'm Carrie Adler. I work for Mr. Frank Evans."

"Well, welcome luv," said Ted. "Good luck 'ere, dear. I 'ave to go ter Mr. Evan's office. 'es got a bit of a problem wiv a plug that aint workin' which I need to make right."

"Do you know where he went?"

"Yep, Ruby, 'is secretary, told me to get over there and get it all done while 'e was away."

"Did she say where he went?"

"Yep, he's visitin' shops for a few days all round London to check on stuff. Somethin' like that."

"Oh, I see," said Carrie, her eyes lighting up.

"I must be off. Nice meetin' you. If you need anythin' fixed, just dial me number," said Ted, writing it on a piece of scrap paper he took from his trouser pocket.

"Thank you," said Carrie, watching Ted grab his mug.

"So that's where he is. I'm so relieved. I thought he might have had an accident," she said to herself. Pushing the chair under the table, she joined the queue. Looking over the menu, she decided on a snack for Regina, then went back to the office.

"Here. Enjoy."

"Thanks, it's just what I needed. I'm famished," said Regina.

"By the way, I just found out where Frank is."

"You did?"

"I met the janitor."

"Oh, Ted? He's all over the place here, and knows the goings on. So what did he tell you?"

"Frank's traveling around London checking on the shops we sell our woolens to."

"Oh, that's good. He usually tells us he'll be away."

"Well, I better get back to see if someone has come to my desk with more work."

"You can be sure of that. Ruby will be sending stuff. She does that when Frank goes somewhere."

On the desk was a note from Ruby, stating that the information she had left must be sent to their customers in Canada explaining the new cashmere models would be available in the spring, and Yamzing's was ready to accept future orders.

"Oh, I better start in." Carrie set to work on her computer. She didn't look up till lunch time when she saw the employees leave. Not feeling hungry after her snack, she stood up and stretched. Picking up her mirror, kept in her desk, she studied her necklace that set off her special dress. "Damn," she uttered. "I put on my red dress just for Frank, and he isn't here to see it." But it was then she made up her mind she would go out with him for that cup of tea if he asked.

Thirty-Three

The Grandchildren

Janet and Ron Rosen waited patiently at Miami International Airport for the arrival of their grandchildren from Twinsburg, Ohio. Escorted to the gate, they located seats. Sitting there, Janet crossed and uncrossed her legs, and continued staring at her watch.

"Janet, get that troubled look off your face; the plane will be close to time. They'll be here soon. I can't wait to see them. Bet they've grown a couple of inches."

"I'm sure of that."

The plane landed, and it wasn't long before they greeted their grandchildren. A chaperone brought them over.

"Thank you so much for caring for our grandchildren," said Janet.

"Your welcome," she answered. "They were good travelers."

Elated, Ron hugged Joey and Jennie, then Janet kissed them. "Ready for the Skylight Inn?" asked Ron, taking them to find the luggage.

"Yeah," they chimed in.

Janet at first had refused to go along with Sue's plans to visit the Skylight Inn during the holiday season, but Sue had made a decision not to give up. Being persistent, she contacted Ron after explaining how important it was to carry out Sarah's wishes by having the children learn their heritage and the two religions. Sue reminded Ron the children had visited Florida since they were babies, and it was a tradition that ought to continue. Finally, Ron saw that Sue made sense and convinced Janet the divorce must not interfere with the children's lives. Janet eventually agreed to put aside her feelings. She made the effort to get together with Sue and Al for the annual family reunion.

When Ron saw Jennie, he beamed and held her close. Jennie's red hair and blue eyes were the image of his beloved daughter. His heart beat faster. Walking through the airport, with his grandchildren strolling alongside him, Ron's face wore a perpetual grin. Joey began pumping his grandfather with questions. "Are we going to swim in the ocean?"

"Yes, Joey" said Ron.

"Does that mean we're gonna fish too?" asked Joey.

"Sure it does."

"Will we light the Hanukkah candles and get all those presents like last year," asked Joey.

"Yes, of course," said Janet.

"We will? Yeah!"

"Why couldn't my dad and Matilda come with us? She said she will be with us forever now 'cause she's marrying my daddy," said Jennie.

"That's because they are too busy to make it this time," said Janet with a forced smile and shaking hands. "Grandmother Sue and Grandfather Al are coming here, too. They'll be flying in from California tomorrow."

"Yeah," yelled Jennie, jumping up and down. "Can I have an ice cream?"

"Not now, Jennie. We'll get you something to eat at the Skylight Inn, which isn't far. Wait till you see your rooms. I think you'll like them."

At the family house, Jennie rushed upstairs to her mother's room. She searched for the familiar, but nothing was the same. The room had pink walls with a canopy bed and a bedspread decorated with

Walt Disney characters. In the middle of the bed was an American doll. On a white dresser with a large oval mirror sat a new comb and brush set. Around the walls were her mother's paintings.

"This is your room now," said her grandmother. "Your mother would have liked you to have it. No one else will sleep here, Jennie, so whenever you come and visit, it'll be waiting for you."

Jennie picked up the doll and spun around the room. "Oh, I love it, grandma."

"Good. Let's find Joey and show him his room." Janet peered down the staircase to see Ron and Joey ascending.

"Here's the boy that wants to see his bedroom," said Ron.

"Right this way, Joey," said Janet. Joey entered the room to see framed prints of famous baseball players, and on his bed was a new baseball bat and ball. On one wall facing the bed was a self portrait of his mother. Joey touched it and stood silently. He closed his eyes. Being the oldest, he remembered the day his mother had died and how beautiful she was. Though he bravely held back the tears, the pain he felt at the loss of his mother remained. It had been Matilda who had helped him heal. For a moment he put his hand over his eyes, then opened them and looked at the prints.

"Oh, boy, Jackie Robinson, my favorite," he said, staring at the print. "Can I try out the bat and ball now? Will you play a game?"

"Sure," said Ron as Joey ran down the stairs with Ron following. After the game, they all washed up and got ready for supper. After dinner, the children bathed and Janet took them up to bed for an early night. Feeling tired after an exciting day, Janet sat in the living room with Ron. She looked over at him and smiled. "Do you know you're a wise man?"

"I am? How so?"

"Your decision to bring the children and the Evergreens here was smart. I feel good about the whole thing. Sue's right. How could we not enjoy them together? Our life without our grandchildren would be so empty, a big blah, a big nothing. The Evergreens arrive tomorrow. I'll be planning to take the children for the Hanukkah service at my temple next week. I want the rabbi to meet them, and when Sue gets here she can decide what she'd like to do. She'd probably want to decorate the Christmas tree that Jay brought in last night. It's magnificent. She loves to arrange flowers. What do you think?"

"Think, I'm not thinking, Janet. I'm just enjoying," said Ron, ginning at her.

"It's back to the airport early tomorrow to pick them up. We should get an early night. I'll just check the hotel to make sure the rooms are nice, and they have a good view."

"Good idea, my legs are tired from the baseball workout, but I better get used to it. I promised Joey I'd play again tomorrow."

Thirty-Four

The Celebration

Carrie placed her grandmother's rings on each finger, brushed her hair, did her make-up, and stared in the mirror. Searching through her wardrobe; she pulled out her best navy suit she often wore for job interviews and special occasions.

"This is the day. The two months are up," she yelled out the window, her voice echoing over rooftops. Taking her suit off a hanger, she dressed. Rushing to the kitchen to find her mobile phone, she picked it up and dialed, then she heard her mother's voice. "Mum, where are you?"

"I just got off the bus. Dad and I will be right there. How are you?"

"How am I? Can't you guess? I'm as nervous as a newborn kitten, and I couldn't find my dress shoes."

Carrie flung on her coat and rushed out the door and down the street. There she saw her parents coming toward her. Running, she caught up to them.

"Did you just mark off the last day?" asked her father.

"Oh, dad you know me too well. Of course I did."

"All right then. Let's go meet Mr. Mackintosh," said her father. He looked at his watch. "Our appointment is for ten o'clock. We've plenty of time. We had a good rest at that hotel, but it was bloomin' expensive, just like everything else is in London."

"Dad, don't worry about that. I'm going to pay you back for that expense."

Gary laughed. "You will? That's good."

Arriving at Mr. Mackintosh's, he greeted them and led them to his office where they sat around his large oak desk.

"How's everyone?" asked Mr. Mackintosh. They said nothing, quietly waiting. "Ready? Carrie, here's the document to state the will and inheritance have been turned over to you. It's all legal now. You can take this to the bank, and they'll take care of you. Have you been thinking on how to manage your new income? Do you have any questions that I can help you with?"

Carrie sighed. "I do, but I don't know where to begin yet. Thank you for your guidance. I've appreciated it. I've been planning out what to do, and have thought about the investments you mentioned."

"Carrie, that's good. I'm pleased to hear you've thought things through. I'll be recommending Mutual Funds which I can discuss with you when you're ready."

Gary stared at his daughter. "My mother was right by making you wait the two months to make some decisions. That was so clever of her."

"You think so? Dad, I did do some investigating. I want you to know the first thing I'm doing is signing up for classes toward a degree in business. What do you think?"

"Well, that's great."

"Will you be leaving your job?" asked her mother.

"I might have to."

Mr. Mackintosh got up from his chair. He shook hands with Carrie "Would you like to make an appointment to get you going with the investments?"

"Yes," said Carrie, feeling her body tremble.

"All right, let me check my calendar."

With the appointment made, Gary thanked him for his assistance, and the three walked out of Mr. Macintosh's office to the bank.

"That's a relief," said Rita. "Your inheritance is safely in the bank."

"Yes, it is, Mum. I had only five pounds in my checking account, and I was getting edgy."

"Really, that was not a good thing to have gotten it so low," said her mother, her voice getting louder.

"Well, I don't have to worry now."

"I hope not," said her mother in an anxious voice.

"Okay, I'm ready for celebrating," said Gary

"Me, too," said Rita.

"I counted the hours and couldn't eat just thinking about today, but I feel hungry now," said Carrie.

Rita laughed. "Are you going to be okay, Carrie?"

"Okay, Mum? I'm ecstatic."

Gary gave his daughter a serious look. "Where did you put Mr. Mackintosh's card for the appointment?"

"I have it safely in my wallet. I plan to listen to him with regard to the investments, but I'm going to do other things."

"What are they, Carrie?" asked her mother.

"I plan to have some fun."

"I know that," said her father." I hope not too much. You'll need to watch over that money as carefully as you can."

"Dad, you're acting stuffy. It's not like you at all."

"Maybe I'm changing. Your mother and I are just concerned about your welfare. That's all."

"Can we go have lunch now?" asked Carrie, with a blank look.

"Lead the way. You know the best places," said her mother.

"How about taking a ride up West for a real celebration? Come on, I'll take you to Charlene's where Anne works. The food is the best. They have a super menu."

"You mean you'll have Matilda's mother wait on us?"

"Of course not, I'll get the manager to let Anne join us. I want to share my great day with her too."

"How are you going to do that?"

"I'll give him a big tip."

Her parents laughed as they walked to the bus stop. Carrie sat on the bus between her parents. "Ready for the West End," she asked, "and maybe go shopping after lunch?"

Thirty-Five

Making Plans

After meeting with her parents, settling her inheritance, and having a delicious dinner with Anne, Carrie sat on her sofa underneath a pole lamp with a bright light, staring at her new Individual Bank Account. "This is really mine. Oh, I have so much to learn," she said, getting up, yawning, then putting her new identity bank card at the bottom of her jewelry box.

She thought of what she wanted to do. She knew she desired a bigger flat so she could bring Oscar to stay with her. Larger rooms and more closet space was something she'd dreamed of, but had worried about the cost, but now she knew she could look for a larger flat. She decided that during the week she would call for an appointment at the London Business School to arrange a time to sign up for classes for the new semester.

Locating a sheet of paper she began writing. After jotting down her ideas, she put the paper on the kitchen counter. "Oh, it's impossible to decide on what to do first. I'll have to call Mr. Mackintosh tomorrow and have him help." With her decision made, she put on the kettle for a cup of tea. She found the biscuits in her old fashioned tin box given to her by a friend. Relaxing, she drank the tea and watched Pete singing in his cage. "Pete," she said, "You are so much company."

Just as she was finishing her tea, her cell phone rang. Feeling sleepy, she decided not to answer. It stopped ringing and then the ringing began again. This time she picked up the phone.

"Hello, Carrie, I tried all day to get you but couldn't reach you. I suppose you were out. It's me, Matilda. I hope I haven't called too late to congratulate on your inheritance. I'm so happy for you."

"Matilda, it's wonderful to hear your voice. Yes, my inheritance. It has been so surprising. How are you?"

"I'm fine now that the divorce is over. It was so draining. I feel relieved. Richard and the children are doing really well, and I'll be through with my student teaching in the spring and plan to get married then, but I'm sure my mother told you that."

"She did."

"Are you coming to my wedding?"

"I planned to, but wasn't sure of the date. Only now I've decided to attend business school, so it might not be possible to come. It will depend on the spring break here, but you have inspired me to learn. I'm sorry Matilda."

"Oh, that's such good news that you are going back to college, and I do understand. But there's nothing like learning. My education at the university has been hard but worth it. It's been a wonderful experience. I just wanted you to come. I miss you Carrie, and I'm getting homesick. I'd like to get to London during the summer and bring my whole new family. I so want to show you the Cleveland area. It's a great city with lots to do. You'll love the Rock and Roll of Fame Museum and the theater section."

"Sounds fantastic, I miss you too," said Carrie. "I'll get to visit you, but as I've said, spring might not be possible. I'll let you know when, and we'll talk again soon. Bye, bye." Hearing the phone click, Carrie sat there reminiscing. Her friend's voice brought a huge smile to her face. She put the dishes in the sink and threw out her teabag.

"I'm tired. What a day this has been," she said, yawning.

She approached Pete's cage. He sat on his swing singing. "Pete, it's time to call it a night."

"Night, Pete. I'm off to bed, so your singing must cease," she said, covering his cage. Changing into her nightgown, she fell on her bed, hugging her pillow, and was soon in a deep sleep.

Thirty-Six

An Education

Frank Evans sat at his desk attempting to get organized after his business trip. A tap on the door disturbed his concentration.

"Come in." Ruby entered with a mug of coffee.

"How's everything here going?" he asked. Any problems while I was away?"

"No. I have the results of the raffle tickets. Brian took care of everything. Here you go," said Ruby handing him the money and the list of names of those who entered. "Here's the coffee. It's real hot."

"Thank you, Ruby. It's just what I needed. Looks like plenty of tickets have been sold," he said. "Send a memo to our employees and thank them for their hard work. Anything else needing my attention?"

"I've some papers that require your signature. I forgot to have you sign them before you left. Sorry."

"Okay, Ruby, I'll take care of them now."

"And, oh, one more thing, Carrie Adler will be coming in. I gave her an appointment to speak to you at two p.m."

"Did she say what it's about?"

"No. she just asked for a time when she could see you."

"All right, thanks, Ruby."

Frank sat back and examined the papers awaiting his signature. He'd visited London shops, and had the owners display Yamzing's products in their windows. He felt pleased with the window displays and to have learned that the new styles were selling well. He tapped a pencil on his desk and looked around his office. Sweeping his hair off his forehead, his mind focused on Carrie. He liked her, and wondered why she needed to see him. There was a spark about her, and each time he saw her, he became more enamored. He wondered why Carrie had made a formal appointment to see him, and hoped she was not having a problem. "Well." he uttered. "I'll soon find out."

At her desk, Carrie kept glancing at her watch, wondering how she was going to ask for a part time position. She had met a counselor at the business college and signed up for classes for the winter, beginning in January and ending in May. But she still wanted her job and knew half the reason for this was she liked Frank. She was afraid if she left, she might not see him again. But even now, she was unsure what she would say to him. She took out her small mirror in the desk drawer and touched up her makeup and combed through her hair. Relieved she had made the decision to begin classes, she stood up. Picking up her bag, she walked over to Ruby's office.

Ruby looked up. "Hello, Carrie, Mr. Evans is expecting you. Go right in."

"Thanks," said Carrie, tapping on the door.

"Come on in, Carrie," said Frank. "How are you?" he asked as she stepped in.

"Just fine, thank you."

"What can I do for you today?"

"Well, I," said Carrie, trying to find the right words.

"Carrie, is there something the matter?"

"No, no. It's just this. I've signed up for business classes which will begin in a fortnight. I'm returning to business school to better myself and seek out a career. What I'm trying to say is that I won't be able to work full time and if it's possible to stay on and work in a part time position? I do enjoy working for this company."

Frank pulled his chair closer to the desk. "That's a surprise," he said, his eyebrows rising. "I like having you here. Are you sure about this? We often have promotions, and are always interested in capable people, and I've already considered you to be that!"

Carrie felt a warm glow. The compliment was like a lightning bolt going through her. "Oh, thank you," she said, feeling her stomach twinge.

"I thought that after working here a year, you could have a chance of a promotion."

"Oh, that's really great, but I've decided to work at my goal."

"Okay. I can find you another position in our company. I'll have to investigate where your talents could be used. We'll miss you. How about joining me for a cup of tea at the deli? You can tell me more then. Now, don't turn me down. I'm sure you have lots more to share."

"Oh, that would be just great," she said, smiling.

"Good. I have a weakness for bagels and cream cheese."

"I love bagels," said Carrie.

She got up. He caught her hand and shook it.

"You have a strong handshake."

"I do. That's because of all that weight lifting at that gym. It also means I'm worthy. What do you think?"

"I think you're right. Shall I meet you at the deli say in twenty minutes?

"Yes, I'll look forward to it."

Leaving Frank's office, Ruby took off her glasses and stared at Carrie. "Is everything okay?"

"Yes, thank you," said Carrie, practically waltzing to her desk. She sat a moment and then dialed Brian's extension and told him the news. He wished her good luck, and they promised each other they would keep in touch. Carrie tidied up her desk and then went to the bathroom. She freshened up and then took off to the deli to meet Mr.

Frank Evans, who she would now address as Frank. She felt her heart skip a beat and her face flush with excitement.

Thirty-Seven

The Winner

Josh Smith came home from his Saturday card club game. Most Saturdays after meeting with his polka friends he entered the house with a defeated look, but this time he came in beaming. He looked at Anne sitting in her favorite chair cuddling Nifty.

"You look comfortable. Hey, I've won for a change," said Josh, showing Anne the pound notes, flicking and counting them with his fingers and thumb. "Are you ready to go out this evening for dinner and celebrate my good fortune?" he asked, kissing her.

"Why that's wonderful," said Anne putting Nifty down. "I'm glad. Where do you want to go?"

"I dunno. Some place you'd like."

"Okay, I'll put the meat back in the fridge."

"It won't spoil?"

"No."

"Good. Go get ready."

Anne rushed to the bathroom, and then entered her bedroom. She searched her closet and came out twirling in a green print long dress.

"You look gorgeous. I like the combination. Where did you get that dress?"

"Oh, the dress, I got it on sale a while back. And I bought the bracelet from a waitress at work who makes jewelry as a hobby. There's always someone selling something at Charlene's. I try to support the staff. Everyone works hard, and they help me out when I need it. Glad you like it."

"That's nice to do that. Did you go shopping with Carrie this afternoon?"

"No. I went on my own. I missed her company. She has to study lots these days, and the latest news is she's going with her boss to see Shania Della sing at the Palm Jazz night club. Remember, I told you about Shania. Carrie met her at that tennis club. It'll be next Saturday night, so please don't make other plans. There'll be her family and friends supporting her. Carrie has said she has a marvelous voice. She sings jazz, which I love, and I know you like that kind of music."

"I do. I recall you mentioning her. Who's Carrie's boss?'

"I've told you. It's Frank Evans. He's the one that rushed Carrie to the hospital when she collapsed at her desk."

"Yes. I remember. I'll look forward to meeting him. Carrie's made a big change in her life. I suppose it's to do with her getting that inheritance."

"It is. Going to college is what she will do first, which is a good thing. She seems serious about being a student, so it looks like she's going to learn how to manage her money. I'll see what she has to say next week."

"Emily and Jim are coming over tomorrow. She's bringing over her mix breed rescue dog. We'll have to keep Nifty out of the way. We could have a war. Emily wants to show us her new designs too. She's got herself a few good customers. I'll give Eric a ring when we get back to the flat. I want him to come over and spend Sunday with all of us."

"Sunday, I'll be going to the cemetery to visit my wife's grave. It would have been her birthday tomorrow. I'll be going in the morning."

"I'll go with you. I'll say some prayers and take along a pot of fresh flowers. They won't be here until the afternoon, so we should have plenty of time. The only problem is I haven't done my usual shopping. After dinner we'll need to get some groceries. I haven't baked in ages, so we'll pick up something from the bakery."

"Something? Are you joking? I know it'll have to be a chocolate cake."

"Josh, you are right as usual."

"I am. That's good. It looks like we'll have a busy Sunday."

"We will, but it'll be great seeing them. I hope to hear good news from Jim and his job."

"He mentioned last time that he's been selling a lot of new Fords, and he likes being a manager."

"What about Eric? He hasn't called lately."

"All I know is he's running back and forth with his lorry doing all that electrical work and repairing wiring in those old houses that have been remodeled since the Olympic Games. The whole bloody area has been rebuilt! The East End is fantastic with all those new skyscrapers. Let's go to a fancy pub for dinner there. It's becoming like the West End, with tourists taking it all in. We'll catch up with Eric on Sunday if he gets here. I think he's still dating that Betty. I wish he'd bring her over. I want so much to meet her. He's a good son and has been the backbone of Matilda's education."

"Yes, you're right about that. All right, the East End is where we'll go. I could do with a pint of beer. Does Nifty need anything before we go?"

"No, he's had plenty to eat today."

"Right love, to the East End we go."

Thirty-Eight

The Nightclub

Carrie had shopped for a new dress to wear for Shania's presentation at the Palm Jazz night club. She had chosen a long purple gown and the costume jewelry inherited from her great-grandmother. Gazing in the mirror, she felt pleased. The jewelry set off her dress. She sprayed an expensive perfume behind her ears. Dancing around the room, she knew that many women would see her and wish they were wearing her exotic dress. Most of all, she knew that Frank would be beguiled.

Carrie had begun working part-time and dating Frank Evans, enjoying every moment she spent with him. She felt comfortable with Frank. His knowledge of the world gave her insight on things she never thought about. She had never been in love, but now all she could think of was of Frank Evans. Looking at her watch she saw it was eight o'clock. There was a light tap on the door. Carrie opened it to a smiling Frank.

"Carrie, you look so pretty. Are you sure you aren't making the debut tonight?"

"Oh, I don't think so. I can't sing or carry a tune. The audience would boo me off the stage if I opened my mouth."

Frank grinned. These last few weeks had been good for him. He rarely saw Carrie at the company for she worked in a different department. Office romances were discouraged by company executives, but Frank felt that as Carrie only worked a few hours a week, he wasn't breaking any rules. He saw her as fun to be around, and her quick mind and clever remarks had him enthralled. He had dated many, but a serious relationship was not something he desired. He enjoyed his freedom and his bachelor status, and he wished to keep it that way.

"Ready?" he asked.

"Yes. I'll just get my coat."

They arrived at the nightclub to find a packed audience chatting quietly and waiting for Shania to perform. They located a table close to Shania's family. Her mother waved to Carrie. A waiter came to the table and Frank ordered some beverages.

"I feel the excitement all around," said Carrie.

"I do, too," said Frank admiring the night club.

"Anne should be here somewhere," said Carrie. "I'll see if I can find her." She stood and glanced around the room. She turned to face Frank. "I'll check the tables."

"Okay," said Frank, looking toward the stage.

"Good evening, ladies and gentlemen. Welcome to the Palm Beach Jazz Club," said the conductor. "This evening I'd like to introduce you to Shania Della, a lovely young jazz singer. Let's welcome her," he said enthusiastically.

Carrie dashed back to the table. "Oops, I made it back in time. Josh and Anne are sitting over on the other side near the stage. They've got the best seat to see her. I'll introduce you to them later."

"Good," said Frank, pulling his chair to a spot to get a better view of Shania.

"Ladies and gentlemen, this evening Shania's going to sing some songs that Lena Horn made famous," said the conductor. He left the stage and a spotlight beamed on Shania. She opened up with "Honey Suckle Rose" and ended with "From This Moment On." All together, she sang six songs. Among them was Lena Horn's most famous,

"Stormy Weather." At the end of her performance the audience stood and applauded.

"Wasn't she wonderful?" gasped Carrie.

"Yes, I'm impressed," said Frank.

Carrie joined Shania's mother. Carrie congratulated her. At the table, voices murmured happily and clinking glasses celebrated Shania's performance.

"She did good," said Shania's mother. "I'm so proud."

"She did," said Carrie, hugging her. "Okay, I'm going back to the table, and hope I can talk to Shania later."

"Fine," said Mrs. Della.

The band began playing some famous pop music. "Come on, Carrie, let's dance this one," said Frank.

"I'd be delighted." She rested her cheek on his as they slowly danced.

Josh and Anne came on the floor. Dancing past Carrie, she winked. "My, they make a lovely couple," said Anne to Josh.

"Yes, they do," said Josh whirling Anne around.

"It's been a lovely evening."

"I'd say; I had no idea that Carrie had such a talented friend. She's going to go a long way. I bet she'll be recording soon."

"I can believe that," said Anne.

Around two in the morning Frank escorted Carrie back to her flat. He kissed her good night. Smiling, she unlocked the door, threw down her handbag, hung up her dress, then headed to the bathroom "This was a perfect evening," she said washing her face in the bathroom sink. It seemed almost like a dream."

Leaving the bathroom, she approached Pete's cage, took him out and kissed him on the head. "Pete, how are you?" she asked, and then she put him back in the cage. "Go back to sleep, Pete. It's bed for me."

Thirty-Nine

Hello Nifty

With the spring semester over, Carrie had earned her first college credits at London's Business School; and here it was the first week in June. Having missed Matilda's wedding in April, she had contacted her and said she would visit after her vacation in Miami Beach, Florida. Sitting at her dressing table, she stared at her unmade bed. She pulled out her passport. Looking it over, she tried to remain calm, but she felt an excited bubble bursting within. In one week she would be off to Miami Beach. Visualizing the beach, sand, and the ocean, she sat motionless. Startled by the phone ringing, she jumped up and rushed to the kitchen.

She heard Anne's voice. "Carrie, it's me; can you come over?"

"Anne, what's wrong? You sound worried."

"I am. It's Nifty. He's not eating and barely moving. I called the veterinarian. Could you come with me to his appointment? Josh is working late, and I'm a wreck."

"I'll be over as soon as I can," she said, putting her passport in a kitchen drawer.

Carrie arrived at Anne's flat to find her walking about the room with Nifty limp in her arms.

"I'm so relieved you could get here. If you worked full time, I'd be stuck, and by the looks of things I need to get Nifty to the vets before it closes. Thanks for getting here so fast. Okay, help me put him in the carrier. Last time Josh took him to Eric's it was nothing but a nightmare getting him into that thing."

This time Nifty barely moved when Carrie opened the carrier. Seeing Nifty with no spark to him, she stared helplessly. "Don't worry, Anne; he probably has some kind of a bug that's going around."

"We'll soon find out," said Anne, trembling.

At the vets, Anne and Carrie waited for the technician to call them to the office. When the doctor appeared, Anne told him that Nifty had not been himself for two days, and he wasn't eating.

"Okay, let's look him over," said the doctor. "He hasn't a fever, and as he is an older cat, we'll need to check him out for different maladies he might have. Leave him here for tonight, and we'll give him a blood test and have the result completed by tomorrow afternoon."

"Oh, I suppose it'll be best to do that," said Anne.

"Yes, it is," said the veterinarian.

"Thank you," said Anne as she and Carrie left the office.

"Come on. I'll take you somewhere for a cup of tea, Anne. You look all in."

"No, I just want to go home. We can have tea at my flat. I'm so grateful you came with me. Nifty has never been ill, except for that terrible accident, which left him in such a state. He's been just fine, and to see him like this is awful." With those words, Anne burst into tears.

"Anne," said Carrie. "I'm sure the doctor will help him. Let me put the kettle on, and we can have a strong cup of tea."

Above the new black refrigerator, Carrie saw Anne's favorite teapot. "I know my way around your kitchen so you just sit there and I'll brew the tea," she said, picking up the old china teapot.

Anne wiped her red eyes while Carrie poured the boiling water into the teapot over the tea leaves and let it brew.

"Here we go. That tea you have looks to be delicious."

"I do like it. And so does Josh," said Anne, blowing her nose. "I suppose I am getting carried away. I have to have some patience, but I can't imagine my life without Nifty. Bloody hell, he's been through so much."

"He has, but look, he made it."

The two drank their tea. "Anne, I'm leaving next week for Miami Beach. You haven't forgotten have you? I'll be at the Skylight Inn for two weeks, and then I'll be off to visit with Matilda and Richard."

"That's right you will. It's like you're taking my place. I'm grateful you're going. Be sure to bring me back all the news. Matilda will be tickled pink to see you, but won't you be missing Frank Evans?"

"I will of course, but he knows I planned the trip a long time ago."

"Is your relationship serious?"

"I'm not sure about that."

"Really, I'm surprised. You seem so smitten with him."

"I am, but that's about it for now."

"Oh, I see. I had better stop prying."

"Good," said Carrie. "Is there anything special you want me to take to Matilda?"

"Yes. I have a new photo of Nifty. I'll get it from my desk."

Calmly, Anne returned with a picture of her beloved cat and gave it to Carrie. "Here, doesn't he look absolutely gorgeous?"

"There's no question about that. She can put it in frame."

The front door opened and Josh entered. "Hey, you two, what's going on?"

"I m just drinking the best cup of tea I've had in ages. Do you want one?" asked Carrie.

"Yes. How come you're pouring the tea?"

"Oh," said Carrie. "I'm helping Anne out."

Anne put her cup down. "Josh, Carrie came over to help me take Nifty to the vets. You know how he's been these last couple of days, and he seemed so much worse. He's not himself. I didn't want to bother you at work. He's there for the night. They're watching over him and giving him blood work, and will call in the morning with the results."

"He'll be all right," said Josh, reaching for Anne's hand.

"I think he'll be okay too," said Carrie.

"I hope you're both right," said Anne. "I just have to convince myself he'll get well."

Forty

It's Florida

Frank arrived at Carrie's flat and rang the doorbell. "Are you all set?" he asked, greeting her.

"Yes, I am. I think I've got most things organized. I'm still not good at that. Pete's with my mother. I've paid up the rent. I've stopped the newspaper, and the stove is off; so if there is anything else, I hope it's not important."

"That means you're ready. I'm going to miss you. A month away is a long time. What am I going to do without you?"

"Oh, you'll be so busy. You'll hardly know I'm gone."

"That's not true. I'm beginning to realize I can't imagine my life without you, so much so that I don't want you to leave. Who am I going to tell my rotten jokes to and laugh with?"

"For one month, I'm sure you'll think of something," said Carrie, beaming. "We better get going, but I must call Anne and see how Nifty is."

"Okay," said Frank, swallowing hard.

Carrie dialed Anne's number. "Hello, Anne. How's Nifty?" she said, pleased to have caught her at home.

"Thank you for calling, Carrie. He's on a kidney medication and a special prescription cat food. It looks like this will help. He seems better. The doctor thinks the medication will help, but his kidneys are not good, so I think it will be a matter of time for my Nifty. Tell Matilda that he's fine."

"I'm sorry, Anne. I'll be sure to tell Matilda only good news."

"Carrie, you take care of yourself. Enjoy Miami Beach. I know you can't wait to swim in the ocean."

"You know me. I love that beach and the hotel. I was thinking how much the children will be happy to have their nanny back. Matilda loves those kids so much. They are lucky to have her."

"You're right. She never wanted to leave them. It's strange how things worked out. Now she's their step-mother. I just hope she's happy with Richard. It's been quite a year for us," sighed Anne. "Take care of yourself and behave."

"I'll try. I'll see you in a month." Carrie pushed her mobile phone to off. "I'm ready to leave," she said, collecting her suit cases.

"I'll take those," said Frank. At the airport, he said goodbye to Carrie as she entered the gate to catch her plane to Miami National Airport. He had held her close and wished her safe trip. He felt lonely watching her walk away. He stood a while, and then walked through the airport to the underground train station to catch a train that would take him back to work. He thought that Miami Beach was too far away and hoped that Carrie would miss him.

At the Skylight Inn, Miami Beach, Carrie sat in the Rose Restaurant eating a late dinner. She gazed at the fountain and the tourists gathering. The décor was different from her last visit. Goldie, who had returned from Ohio and to her waitress position, told Carrie that Mark had rearranged everything, and his sister Sarah's paintings were displayed in the new restaurant.

Now, comedians' photos dotted the walls. Carrie liked the photograph of Jerry Seinfeld. His way of telling a joke made her laugh. Sitting there, she immersed herself in the captivating expressions of these famous comics. Her eyes caught a handsome young man coming toward her. It was Aaron Rosen.

"Good evening, I'm Aaron. You looked familiar. You were

Matilda's bridesmaid, right? You're Carrie."

"Yes, that's me. I was her bridesmaid, but that's a sore subject; isn't it?"

"True, it is around here. What brings you to Miami Beach?"

"Oh, it's really quite simple. I fell in love with the surroundings and your lovely hotel which I planned to come back to the minute I could afford to stay here. After my first visit, it left an impression on me. Are you surprised that I came, considering the circumstances?"

"Well, it's not your fault that the marriage is over. There's nothing that can be done about that, but I'm pleased you decided to visit us. May I bring you coffee? Our chef has made a delicious chocolate cheese cake. Would you like a slice?"

"No, thank you. Goldie is bringing me a snack and a cold drink."

"Okay, let me know if I can be of service to you. We have some nice tourist sites. I can show you around."

"Oh, that would be very nice, thank you."

Goldie brought the coffee, and Carrie chatted to Aaron. She began yawning. "I suppose my trip has caught up with me. I feel sleepy. I'm ready for that luxurious bed. I'll have to say good night, Aaron."

"Fine, traveling can be tiring. Have a good sleep, and welcome to our hotel."

"Thank you. I'm looking forward to viewing the ocean from my suite while having breakfast tomorrow morning."

"Your suite is one of the best we offer. You'll be enthralled with the view. Okay, I'll call you late morning to see if you want a ride around Miami Beach. You can see a lot on the Miami Trolley. Tourists like it."

"I have to get to the beach first, so maybe I'll make the trolley later."

"Okay, I'll call you in the morning."

After breakfast and a shower, Carrie headed for the beach wearing her new yellow bikini. She carried her suntan lotion, a magazine, towels, and a pillow. Laying back on a deck chair, she gazed at the sea and allowed her mind to go blank.

"This is heaven," she said, watching the plunging waves pressing forward. "At last I'm here." She closed her eyes. Dozing awhile, she awoke to see the tide drifting inward. After moving her umbrella from the edge of the beach, she picked up the magazine and read, then took a stroll to the ocean.

Floating on her back, she felt the warmth of the water. She then came out of the ocean, dried herself, and took to the beach to search for some unusual sea shells. She watched the children with their parents building sand castles, and people smiling and soaking their feet in the waves. Returning to the shelter of her umbrella, she found herself saying, "This is the place for everyone to heal." Looking up, she saw Aaron standing there smiling at her.

"Hi, Carrie. I tried calling you, but had no luck. I thought I'd find you here. How's the beach?"

"Oh, you surprised me. It's everything I'd thought it would be."

"Good. I'm taking a little break. I'm just about through with my apprenticeship. I can now say I'm a chef, so I've earned a break for a few days. Have you thought about the trolley ride? I can take you on a tour this afternoon?"

"Okay, it sounds like something I'd enjoy. Thank you for inviting me."

"My pleasure," said Aaron. "I'll pick you up at your suite around two. Enjoy the beach."

"I am already," said Carrie, pleased that she had been so accepted, and appreciated Aaron's attention. She watched him leave then lay back on the deckchair.

Forty-One

Adamant Ron

It was mid-morning. Ron Rose sat in his office, smiling; he felt as contented as a purring cat. "At last," he thought. "Mark is at the handle of the Skylight Inn. It's taken six months for him to recover. That trip to Spain was what helped, and Goldie is back making Mark smile. What could be better? He has stayed with us. What a relief," said Ron, assembling his business mail in individual piles on his desk. He yawned, stretched, and stood up. He decided to take a brief break and stroll among the flower gardens and then stop at the lobby of the Skylight Inn. It was here he liked to talk to the tourists. As it was off season, he felt it important to keep the tourists happy and advise them on the best places to tour at reasonable prices.

Puffing his cigar, he hoped none of his family would spy on him. He did not want to hear how he ruined the flowers with his cigar butts. Reaching the hotel lobby, he squashed out the end of his cigar with the heel of his shoe and entered the lobby to find Aaron and Carrie selecting pamphlets and post cards of touring areas.

"Well, well, who do we have here, Aaron?" asked Ron. Staring at Carrie, knowing he had met her, but couldn't remember where. Then he knew. "You were Matilda's bridesmaid."

Carrie smiled and shook Ron's hand. "Hi, Mr. Rosen, I was."

"Why have you come to my hotel? Why are you here? Don't you know my son Mark has suffered immeasurably since his divorce from your friend? I think it best that you check out right away. I don't want you to stay here."

"Dad, don't. Carrie likes our hotel and planned to visit with us a long time ago. The divorce has nothing to do with her. It's not her fault."

"True, but I don't want Mark to see her. He's doing well now, and Carrie, you must understand that you being here would have a bad effect on him."

"Oh, my God," said Carrie.

"I can recommend another hotel further down the beach and have Aaron take you there."

"Dad, you're being ridiculous. Mark is all right; he can't hide from people who are friends of Matilda. He's over his divorce"

"Don't you know since Goldie returned to the Skylight, he's been dating her?"

"He is? No, I didn't know that."

"He is Dad. It's true."

"If it's all right with you, Mr. Rosen, I'd prefer to stay."

"After what Aaron just said, I suppose it's possible," said Ron, appearing calmer.

"I'm giving Carrie some pamphlets on sites she can visit," said Aaron.

"How long were you planning to stay?" asked Ron.

"It'll be a fortnight, which means two weeks British time, and Aaron has offered to take me on a trolley ride."

"Since when have you become a chaperone?"

"Since yesterday," said Aaron. "I'm having a break now that I'm through with my internship."

"I've nothing else to say. Okay, enjoy your visit," said Ron apologetically.

Ron returned to his office frowning. There were deep lines across his forehead. They seemed to have increased since worrying about Mark. He wished the chapter of Matilda to close. He felt he had seen enough pain on Mark's face and could stand no more.

In his office, he called out to his secretary. "Hilda, come in. We need to talk. Hurry, get in here."

Turning off her computer, she rushed to Ron's office. "What's wrong?" she asked. "You look like death."

"I'm okay. I just had a sort of a surprise, a shock you might call it."

"What happened?"

"It's Matilda's friend, Carrie. She has come here to vacation."

"Oh, I remember her, a real lively young woman. She loved our hotel, and I recall her telling me she would come back here as soon as she had the funds. She must have gotten the money. Good for her. She has good taste."

"She did? That's what she told you?"

"Yes, I remember her words. Why are you worried about her being here?"

"It's Mark. I don't want him to see her."

"Oh, I wouldn't worry about that. He's okay now. It's been six months since he went through the divorce. It's June, almost summer. He's doing just fine, now."

"How do you mean?"

"I've seen him with Goldie taking walks with her and holding her hand."

"You're the second person who has told me that. How come I didn't know?"

"I've no idea," said Hilda. "I'm glad Carrie made it back here. She told me when she had enough money she would visit our hotel, and it seems she has."

"Mm, I suppose I don't have to worry."

"Of course not. Here, I've brought you these letters to sign. I need to get them off as soon as possible."

"Okay, Hilda. Just don't retire yet."

"I'm not planning on it," said Hilda, leaving the office.

Ron looked about his office, wondering what to do. He tapped his fingers on the desk as though he were playing the piano and hummed a favorite tune. Locating the coffee pot, he filled his cup.

"Maybe Mark is doing all right, after all," he said, slowly drinking the coffee. He got up and began humming an old song.

Forty-Two

Returning Home

On the jet plane back to London, Carrie settled herself in by a window seat. The plane climbed higher, gearing toward its destination, Heathrow Airport. Spotting the cars on the highways surrounding the airport, Carrie thought the cars appeared like little toys drifting along.

Feeling insignificant, she stared at the distant ground below. It was the miracle of jet travel that changed one's life she thought. Thrilled that flying could take her most anywhere, she clipped her safety built to the message of the captain giving directions.

As the hours ticked by, she tried to sleep but could not. She lost interest in the movie and took off her ear phones. Closing her eyes, her mind wandered over her visit to Miami Beach and Twinsburg. She sat there half-awake while the plane floated in and out of the white clouds. Thinking about Florida, she knew it had been exactly what she had wanted. Knowing that her presence at the Skylight Inn had not affected Mark Rosen pleased her. He had stopped by while she ate lunch at The Rose. Welcoming her, he asked her to taste the new fruit dessert, which she had refused. Mark had smiled and asked her how she was doing, and moved on to the next table where he greeted the hotel's other guests.

Matilda, Richard, and the children had escorted her around Cleveland where Carrie visited the theatres, the Rock and Roll Hall of Fame, and museums, which changed her opinion about the Cleveland area. She saw Twinsburg as a good place to live. Sitting back in her seat and feeling cramped her mind wandered to Matilda. Out loud, she uttered, "I hope this marriage lasts." Glancing at a male passenger sitting in the next seat reading a novel, she wondered if he had heard her blurting out her thoughts. He looked up from his book and spoke to her.

"Sorry, I did not hear what you said," he announced in a clear British accent.

"Oh, I was just thinking out loud," said Carrie. "Excuse me."

"I find myself doing that too, at times," said the blond haired young man. "Looks like they are bringing refreshments." He put the book aside and stretched.

"What can I get you?" asked the steward.

"I'd like something cold. Any soda will do," said the man.

"And what can I bring you?" asked the steward.

"A Pepsi if you have it."

Finishing their drinks, the man returned to reading his book. Carrie thought about Frank Evans. He had phoned her in Florida and Twinsburg, and said he would pick her up at the airport, but Carrie had said no. She knew how hectic that would be. The airport would be widely busy which she had stated to Frank. She said she would ring him from her flat. Carrie had decided she could maneuver herself through the London Underground as she was used to traveling and mingling with crowds on her way to work.

Arriving at Heathrow, and after going through customs, Carrie could hardly keep her eyes from closing and was sorry she had told Frank not to come. Instead of taking the trains, she hailed a cab.

Reaching her flat, she left her luggage in the hallway and collapsed on her couch. In seconds she was asleep, still in her wrinkled clothes and shoes. Awakening the next morning at eleven o'clock, she looked down at her feet and laughed. "Oh, my God, I'm a mess," she said, getting up and removing her shoes. "I suppose I'm not much of a traveler."

Checking her mobile phone, she saw there had been lots of calls. "First thing I need is a hot shower and then catch up with the world," she groaned. It was then her phone rang. Grudgingly, she answered.

"Hello."

"Carrie, where are you?"

"I'm home."

"For heaven sakes, why didn't you call me? You said you would the minute you landed."

"Sorry, Mum, I had to go through customs and stuff. I was just too tired after that."

"Oh, are you all right?"

"Yes, perfect. The vacation was so good, Mum. I'll call you back. I'm starving. I have to get myself together. It's groceries first and then phone calls."

"Okay, dear. We'll talk later."

Putting the phone down, Carrie sat a moment. "Well, I better shower," she said, trying to get herself together.

Frank Evans phoned Carrie, but got no answer. He left a message. In the shower, Carrie sang at the top of her voice, and decided to phone Frank as soon as she dressed.

She missed him, and knew she had lots to tell him. Drying herself with a large bath towel, she questioned herself. Was Frank getting serious about their relationship? If so, where did she stand? He had all the requirements she ever wanted in a man, but did she love him? Huddling in her bath towel, she stood still, but her mind was barraged with more questions. "Oh, I'll think about this later," she said, quickly dressing. The phone rang and rang, but Carrie did not answer. She rushed out of the house. It was groceries she needed and breakfast.

It was not until two in the afternoon that Carrie listened to her phone calls. Her parents said they would be bringing back Pete. They mentioned that he had done fine by the kitchen window. Carrie was happy to hear this. After speaking to her family, she phoned Frank.

"Carrie, it's so good to hear from you. I've tried ringing you many times. Where were you?"

"I'm sorry Frank. Coming home was not easy. You don't want to hear how many things I've had to do."

"Are you saying traveling is hard?"

"No, it's me. Well, it is a little tough, and I'm trying my best to become better organized."

"How about dinner this evening, I can pick you up around six?"

"Wonderful," said Carrie hanging up the phone. She felt her stomach churning. "What's the matter with me? I just can't adjust," she said, unpacking her clothes. She put some of her things away then decided to rest. Before she realized it was five o'clock. Panicking, she quickly dressed. Frank picked her up on the dot of six. He swept her in her arms. "I've madly missed you."

"That's good. I'm glad to hear it."

"Ready?"

"I am."

He warmly kissed her and helped her with her jacket. "It's a little chilly."

"I know. I miss the sun already, but am glad to be home."

"Good, let's go."

At the restaurant, Frank reached out across the table and held Carrie's hand. "It seems my life doesn't seem to go well without you. I'm so glad you're back. In his pocket he reached out for a small envelope. "Here look these over."

Carrie opened up the small envelope he handed to her, and two theater tickets dropped out. They were for a West End show, "Mamma Mia."

"Oh," called out Carrie. "What a lovely surprise." She looked at the date.

"It's for next Saturday night. You'll be well rested. I've heard that millions have seen the show. Here, you take care of the tickets. We'll have a lovely evening."

"Yes, we will. Thank you, Frank."

"Carrie, I'm ready for something more. I can't imagine my life without you, so how about marrying me?"

Carrie felt her pulse racing. She stared at him and couldn't fathom what she just heard.

"Well?" asked Frank.

"Oh, Frank, I can't answer that. I so enjoy being with you, but I just can't marry you."

"You can't? Don't you love me?"

"Yes, I do. But I just don't want to marry yet."

"When do you want to marry?"

"In about seven years if you want to wait that long."

"This is a very strange rejection, Carrie, and it doesn't make any sense."

"Frank, please understand. I have personal goals I must meet before I ever get married, and it wouldn't be fair to you. I have to make an attempt at reaching them."

He looked at her and paused. "I'll get the bill and take you back to your flat."

At her door, he held her close, kissed her, then said good night.

"I'll call you in the morning," he said walking away.

Carrie opened her door and felt a choking feeling. She knew she loved Frank Evans, but her future lay before her. She did not feel it wise to tangle up his life. She had often heard the words said that at twenty-one years of age, one's life had just begun.

"I have so much to do," she said, locating her mobile phone. She then dialed the person she most trusted.

Anne picked up the phone. "Well, Carrie, it's about time I heard from you. You've been back a whole day and I've heard nothing. I'm ready to hear about your trip to Florida and Twinsburg and seeing my Matilda."

"Hi, Anne. I do have much to tell you, but it will have to wait until I see you." It was then Carrie started to mumble as she attempted to hold back her tears, but Anne heard the stress in her voice.

"Carrie, Carrie, what's wrong?"

"Carrie, are you ill?"

"No, Anne. I'm okay. I'm just overtired. I need some more sleep. I'll pop around to see you tomorrow evening," she said, gathering herself together. "My parents will be here sometime during the day to bring Pete back. I can come in the evening, if that would be all right?"

"Are you sure you're okay?"

"Yes, Anne. I am. Good night."

"I'll see you then."

Forty-Three

The Future

Josh sat in his favorite chair reading the newspaper. "It's the same terrorist news. That's all we hear these day, and wars all over this world. I can't keep up with it When will all this madness end? I've read enough. I'm going for a walk."

"Don't you want to wait for Carrie? She'll be here soon with the news about her trip,"

"Nah, I'll leave it all to you. You can tell me all about it later."

Josh put on his raincoat and headed for the front door. "I hope it doesn't rain."

"Enjoy your walk," called out Anne as he went along the pathway. Shutting the door, she went to the kitchen and crushed a pill into Nifty's food and fed him.

"There's a good cat. Eat up. That pill seems to be helping you."

The door bell rang, and Anne ran to open it.

"Carrie, it's so good to see you dear. Come on in. I've missed you. Give me your coat." Anne hugged her. "I'll put it in the closet. Come on, sit down. I'm dying to hear everything. I'll make us some tea."

"Don't bother, Anne. I don't want any right now."

"You don't? Are you ready to tell me about your vacation? I want to hear everything."

"It was wonderful. Matilda and Richard gave me a great time and are a loving couple and happy as larks. They told me all about their wedding, and I've brought along some wedding photographs. Sue and Al Evergreen were there. Richard said he was pleased his parents came. He was afraid they wouldn't. He said he needed their support. The children are so happy and are always close to Matilda's side. She gives them lots of attention, and I have to say, they are thriving. The way things seem, I'd say you won't have to worry about Matilda. She's content, but you'll see for yourself if she visits this summer. She said she plans to come."

"She is? Oh, Carrie, you couldn't have given me better news. I so appreciate it. I feel relieved. What about the Skylight Inn? Was it all that you expected?"

"It was fabulous. I went sightseeing, sunbathed, walked along the ocean, rested in the finest suite in the hotel, ate great food, and was escorted around by Aaron Rosen; he's the youngest of the Rosen family. He's a real gentleman. It's a place I never wanted to leave. By the way, Mark Rosen is dating a waitress named Goldie. He was so nice to me and full of smiles. I did hear he was suffering badly from the divorce, but seems okay now."

"Is that so? Tell me more about the lovely Skylight Inn."

"I will later. Once I start, I won't be able to stop."

"Okay, Carrie, now out with what's bothering you. You could hardly talk on the phone yesterday."

"I suppose it's the whole business of marriage. I think it goes back to the day when you called and told me that Matilda was getting a divorce and would eventually marry Richard Evergreen. I have to tell you now that I was shocked."

"I'm sorry you were, and I understand, but Matilda had made a big mistake when she married Mark Rosen. I think at the time she was just flattered."

"It seems she did make a bad mistake. I'll never be ready for marriage."

"You will be when the right man comes into your life."

"I believe I have met the right person."

"Carrie Adler, what are you saying? That is marvelous."

"No, it isn't."

"What do you mean? And who is the lucky man?"

It's Frank Evans, the man who saved my life. He's asked me to marry him, but I said no."

"Oh, my God, Carrie how could you?"

'I've said no because I love him. I know it wouldn't work. I still want to find me. This is the twenty-first century. Women don't rush into marriage like they used to years ago. Now they move in with their partners, and marry when they are around thirty, but moving in is not for me either. Anyway, I've asked Frank if I could make a decision on marriage when I'm older."

"You did? What did he say?"

"He just said he would call me in the morning, and he hasn't. I still need to continue with my education and see the world if I can."

"I see. You've said these things for a long time; so if that's what you want, you must keep that decision. No wonder you were upset when I called. I don't suppose you'll be seeing him now you've refused his offer of marriage."

"We have tickets for a West End show next Saturday night, and I have them."

"Will you still go?"

"It will be up to Frank."

"Are you prepared to lose Frank Evans?"

"No, that's my big problem, and he knows nothing of my inheritance."

"He doesn't? That shows you he loves you for you, and that's good, Carrie. Only you can solve this," said Anne as Carrie's mobile phone rang.

"Hello, Carrie. It's Frank. I've been thinking about us, and I want you to know I'll keep on asking you to marry me. I love you, but I won't rush you. I'll wait for you to give me a date. I'm not giving up."

"Are you sure about this?"

"I believe so. I was twenty-one once. That is young. I love you. I'll just have to find some patience. I'll pick you up for the show on time. But I'll see you before then. Bye darling."

"Who was that Carrie?"

"It was Frank. The show is on and so is my life."

"What do you mean?"

"It means everything is fine."

"It is? Well, that's good."

"I need to make a phone call if you don't mind."

"Sure, I'll be in the kitchen."

"Hello? Oh, Carrie, it's you. You're back!"

"I am Shania, and ready to meet for a tennis game and hear about your singing career."

"I want to hear all about your trip, and I've so much to tell you."

"I have too. See you soon," she said, then pushed her mobile phone button to off. She sat down on Anne's armchair and swept Nifty up.

"How are you today?" she asked the black and white family cat who purred, curling on her lap. "I don't care what Anne says. I just know you're going to be around for a long, long time. Aren't you, Nifty?"

www.ingramcontent.com/pod-product-compliance
Lightning Source LLC
Chambersburg PA
CBHW020437180626
46812CB00003B/1272